No Ordinary Soldier

Ronald Bassett

First published in 1972 by Macmillan London.

This edition published in 2016 by Endeavour Press Ltd.

Table of Contents

Author's Foreword

The China Expedition of 1860 was one of the numerous smaller campaigns fought during the nineteenth century, as part of Britain's 'gunboat policy', which occupy little space in our history books. This is not a specific account of that campaign, but merely of the participation of Rifleman Joseph Dando, whom we have already met in *Dando on Delhi Ridge*.

Dando is not the clinical hero-figure so loved by Victorian writers. He is a very ordinary soldier — one of the thousands of ordinary soldiers that Victorians treated with contempt and abuse, banned from polite society, from theatres and music halls, maintained in squalor and paid with a pittance. Yet these were the men who fought and died to build and defend the biggest empire the world has known and, incidentally, poured the treasures of five continents into the bank-vaults of Britain.

A third of them came from Ireland, the Army's most prolific recruiting ground. Enlistment was marginally better than starvation. Many, too, were illiterate, but they have written pages of glorious history which will live centuries after their bones have crumbled to dust, in Bengal and Burma, the Crimea, Zululand and the Sudan, Abyssinia, Natal, Persia, Ashanti and China. *Ubique*.

1

'It ain't the 'eat,' Rifleman Dando informed Holloran, 'it's the bleedin' 'oomidity.' He wiped the sweat from the creases of his neck with the back of a dirty hand. 'I ain't surprised Chinamen are soddin' yaller, an' wear 'ats like umbrellas.' Every man, said army orders, would land with three days' cooked provisions, 56 rounds of ammunition, greatcoats, full water-bottles, haversacks, and would wear cloth trousers, summer frocks, worsted socks and helmets. There was a full half mile of glutinous Pehtang river mud through which to wade, thigh deep, then seven miles of narrow causeway across the marshes, which could be a death trap if the Chinese artillerymen knew how to lay their guns. It was August, and it had been authoritatively stated that no Europeans could campaign in Northern China after the end of May, when the hot season began, while by November it would be intolerably cold. The British hedged their bets. They had brought Riflemen and Sikhs from India supported by veterans of the Crimea.

Holloran transferred a cud of tobacco from one cheek to the other. 'Shure, an' if there's any place wid more mud than Letterkenny, then it's bloody Pehtang.'

The landscape that met their gaze from the paddle-box of the *Alfred* was not inviting. Below them the river was clay-coloured, floating with filth. Inshore, several armed cutters were taking soundings, and similar small craft threshed between the anchored transports and warships in the estuary — gigs, whalers, lorchas, native sampans, with midshipmen shouting and pipes shrilling. Seaward, in the Gulf of Pechihli, there were more ships, a total of one hundred and fifty. Most were British — *Calcutta*, *Inflexible*, *Furious*, *Actaeon* — but the Tricolour flew at the masthead of the *Audacieuse* and the Stars and Stripes over the massive *Minnesota*. The shoreline was flat, featureless, except for the mazy tumble of rooftops that they had been told was Pehtang.

'If it weren't fer the bleedin' 'oomidity,' Joseph Dando persisted, 'it'd be like takin' cake orf a blind baby.' It was hardly believable that a rag-bag army of Chinamen with umbrella hats, pig-tails, smocks and wooden-soled boots could offer any serious threat to men who had fought at Delhi and Lucknow, the Alma, Balaclava and Sevastopol. Mind, the Goorkhas had looked like Chinamen, with their shaven heads and hair tufts — and the Goorkhas had been savage little bastards.

The *Alfred*'s decks were thickly thronged by riflemen of the 60th and cluttered with stores not yet issued — blankets, bread, butter, bacon, tinned sausages and, under the eye of a sentry, crates of Bass's pale ale from Payne & Co of Calcutta. Butter for soldiers, b'Christ. They'd not had butter in India, only skilly, salt beef, choke-dog biscuit and hard-boiled peas. There'd be not a few long-serving men in the 60th who hadn't tasted butter for more than fifteen years. Things were beginning to change. It was the Crimea that had done it — too late to improve the conditions of the immediately following Sepoy Revolt, but becoming apparent by 1860. The die-hards still growled that stringy beef and choke-dog were good enough for the drunken scum of the Army. Give 'em better and you'll spoil 'em. There were others, like Mr Sidney Herbert and Miss Nightingale, who maintained that soldiers should be allowed at least the same consideration as officers' horses. Even if the butter had already been reduced by the heat to a rancid, yellow oil, it was a start.

Joseph's head was beginning to ache. It usually did after a few hours in the sun. He allowed his fingers to touch the inch-wide scar under his black hair. He shouldn't be alive, Surgeon Innes had said, and wrote to the *Lancet* about it. That had been nearly three years ago, on Delhi Ridge, after they had stormed the Kashmir Gate. He, Dando, remembered the iron-hard *maidan* under his feet as he ran, with the treacherous dawn sun splintering into life behind him, over the Jumna, the wide ditch littered with refuse, and the wall-top wreathed with gun-smoke. Brownlow should be here, he remembered thinking — Tom Brownlow, his rear rank man who had died earlier at Hindoo Rao's house. Then he'd been sprawling, his ears singing and blood in his eyes. A fractured skull, Surgeon Innes had said, with the brain laid bare. Interesting, but of course there was no hope. Not with surgery on a filth-slimed table-top, the flies swarming, and the fetid water from the Nujufgurh Canal that even the gun-mules refused to drink.

But Surgeon Innes had not reckoned with the leather-tough constitution of the little soldier under his scalpel, slum-reared, hardened and immune from years of deprivation and adversity, of bad food and bad water, barrack-room brawls and savage campaigning under inhuman conditions. Dando had confounded the surgeon by surviving. He was bleedin' alive, wasn't he? And now China. Christ, after India, the soddin' pig-tailed Chinamen were goin' ter be easy. As he'd said, like takin' cake orf a blind baby.

The sailors would row them shoreward until the boats grounded. Then, with cartridge wallets hung from necks and rifles carried aloft, they'd wade for the firm ground above high water mark, where the tomb-mounds were. They had charts this time — not like, six years ago, when a British army had blissfully landed in Calamita Bay with nothing better than schoolboy maps and not the slightest knowledge of the Crimean terrain. This time it would be like an exercise on Bagshot Heath, if it wasn't for the bleedin' 'oomidity.

'Move yer arses,' Sergeant Garvin shouted, 'an' git fell in. Holloran, Dando, Rose, Bathurst, Wilson —!' He was looking for the experienced men, the men of Meerut and Ghazi-ud-din-Nagar. 'You'll go in the first boat with Lieutenant Shaw.' He didn't have to tell them to keep their cartridges dry, their Enfields free of mud, but — 'An' keep yer thievin' hands orf private property. There's fifty lashes fer anyone touching booze, an' the same fer monkeying wi' wimmin —' Not that men like these were likely to be impressed by the threat of fifty lashes. Fifty was for boys. Two hundred, now, or three, that'd be different — but fifty was the maximum permitted now. It was like the butter.

'Wimmin,' said Holloran, meditatively. He spat expertly over the side. 'Wid I be telling ye somethin' ye don't know about Chinese wimmin, me ol' Dando?'

Dando grunted, reaching for his rifle. 'Sod orf, Irish. They're jes' shaped different, that's orl. The other way.' He looked towards the distant shoreline, his interest stimulated. 'It'll be a change from some o' them six-inch gun-breeches we 'ad in Bombay.'

2

Among the mountains that fringe Tibet rises the great Huang Ho, the Yellow River, flowing deviously eastward across the broad brow of China until it reaches the sea, to bring, with its sisters Pai Ho and Huai, the sediment of centuries to build the vast alluvial plain that extends over much of the provinces of Honan, Hopei and Shantung. Fertile and easily cultivated, the soil also quickly erodes, dust-like, to choke the rivers, making navigation difficult for all but small craft. It was a terrain knowing devastating floods and searing droughts, times of plenty and times of merciless famine, of populations periodically decimated by starvation, plagues, civil strife and invasion. But it was an enduring, resilient population, like the bamboo bending before the storm but never breaking, multiplying quickly and patiently rebuilding — a fatalist, materialist people who seldom revealed emotion, content with a standard of living that never rose above grinding poverty. It had always been so, for tens of thousands of years.

That there were nations other than Chinese they were aware, but knew almost nothing of them except that they were barbarian, hairy, long-nosed, and all looked alike. The British had the island of Hong Kong, the Portuguese the seedy settlement of Macao, while the other foreign devils, the French, Americans, Russians, had to share the treaty ports of Canton, Shanghai, Amoy, Ningpoo and Foochow, from which it was forbidden to trespass inland.

The Chinese had no desire for foreign influence; they had managed without it for long enough, and the foreigners had little to offer that they wanted. True, China had accepted tobacco from the Philippines, potatoes, maize, peanuts and syphilis from the USA, opium and a few missionaries from Britain. But this was barely scratching the surface of a market so vast that all the mills of Lancashire could not make stocking stuff for the smallest of its provinces. In 1851 British exports to China consisted of only £1½ million of manufactured goods — half of those to Holland — and £6 million of opium. The Chinese condescended to buy Indian bezoar, elephants' bones and teeth for medicinal purposes, rhinoceros horn — an aphrodisiac — kingfisher feathers, tortoise shell, Japan wax, but they preferred bullion. In return they exported thirteen varieties of tea, silk, Spanish Fly, musk, peppermint oil, porcelain, jade and wood carvings. It was difficult to persuade the foreigners that native-made textiles were cheaper and more suitable, that high tariffs placed European goods beyond the reach of most of the people and, in any case, China was self-supporting in almost all the necessities of its teeming peasantry — except in famine areas, of course. And if a million Chinese died annually from starvation, or two million, or three — well, there were many more Chinese.

*

'This is where the bleedin' tea comes from,' Dando told Holloran. 'Did yer know tea comes orf trees?' Holloran did not, but dutifully scanned the distant, bleak mudflats for anything resembling a tea tree. 'Bedad, an' we're foightin' a bloddy war over tay? Last toim ut wuz Indian cartridges, now ut's bloddy Chinamen's tay! Ef ut wuz somethin' *sarious*, loik rum, shure, I'd foight the ol' Dun Cow ev Ballymote — but tay —?'

'There's money in tea,' Dando sniffed. 'There's some people what drink nothin' else. If yer'd been ter Greenwich, yer'd see crates an' crates o' the bleedin' stuff. I reckon' — he waved an arm — 'there's enough tea drunk ter float every one o' them soddin' ships, easy.'

Holloran, who accepted the literal sense of every statement, shuddered at the thought. 'Faith, wud ye belayve ut?' He peered over the gunwale of the wallowing launch. Behind them, on the *Alfred*, the two officers' horses were being hoisted into a waiting scow, and as the crowded launch passed under the stern of the anchored *Minnesota* it met a deluge of good-humoured satire from the ship-confined American sailors at the rails, followed by flung cheroots, plug tobacco and biscuits. 'They speak a *sort* o' bleedin' English,' Dando conceded, 'but it ain't proper. Yer can't expect it.'

'Faith, an' ye can't,' agreed Holloran.

*

It was Britain, the major maritime nation, which spearheaded foreign pressure on China to relax trading restrictions, finally compelling concessions by force of arms in 1842. Other nations watched with interest, aware that Britain did not insist on exclusive rights, and within a few years similar privileges were demanded, and achieved, by the United States, France, Belgium, Sweden, Norway, and Russia.

The new treaty, however, only masked an uneasy truce. China rued her concessions, which indicated loss of face, and in practice there was little improvement in relationships. Britain wanted access to the interior, the legislation of the opium trade, and the establishment of consular residences in Peking, the capital. Again, the other nations watched with interest. What Britain achieved would be a legacy for all. They merely had to sit and wait.

A trivial incident provoked war. In 1856 a small vessel, the *Arrow*, Chinese-owned but registered in Hong Kong and flying the British flag, was boarded by Chinese military in Canton, her crew arrested on a charge of piracy and the British flag hauled down. Later the crew were released, but the British demanded an apology for the violation of her sovereignty, and the Chinese, as ever reluctant to lose face, refused.

Britain had a well-tried, well-drilled answer to this sort of behaviour. It was known as the gunboat policy, and it usually worked. The Royal Navy captured the forts commanding the Canton approaches and bombarded the viceroy's headquarters. Nelson would have approved. The Chinese retaliated by burning down several European warehouses, encouraging unrest in Hong Kong, and even organising the beheading of eleven European passengers on a small British ship by militiamen impersonating mutineers. It was too much. It was tantamount to a declaration of war, and British patience, never a noteworthy quality, was exhausted.

The Crimean War had just ended, and France, like Britain with troops to spare, and pretending justification in the murder of a French missionary, offered to join her erstwhile ally in compelling China to observe European rules of diplomacy. The 'all nations equal' agreement, considered the French, might well be in jeopardy, and a contribution might pay dividends. Britain extended an invitation to the United States to similarly participate, but Washington declined although, as an afterthought, despatched a representative to watch over American interests. Recently at odds with Britain and France, Russia sulked.

During mid-1857 five British regiments were on passage to Hong Kong when, in Bengal, the Sepoy Revolt exploded. Britain's stake in India was immense; China could wait. The troops at sea were diverted to

Calcutta, and their arrival was decisive in tipping the scales against the Indian mutineers.

Within months, however, a combined Anglo-French force had gathered in Chinese waters — 800 British and Indian troops, 2,100 British marines, a Royal Naval brigade of 1,829, and a French naval brigade of 950. Canton was captured, and this time the United States and Russia added their voices to those of Britain and France in demanding revised treaties. The Chinese remained obdurate, and the Allied force moved northward to capture the Taku forts, commanding the approach to Tien-tsin. With Peking itself now threatened, the Emperor capitulated, and the Treaties of Tien-tsin were negotiated.

But the last act was not yet played. The Allies had demanded that the treaties should be ratified in Peking, a city almost unknown to Westerners. The Russian and American ministers accomplished the visit, the latter not without some humiliation, but when the British and French insisted upon proceeding directly to Peking through Tien-tsin — rather than by the less auspicious route designated by the Chinese — they were opposed by force. An attempt to force a passage ended in embarrassing failure, and both British and French sent for reinforcements. The United States and Russia, having achieved their own treaties without firing a shot or expending a single soldier, watched with amusement.

3

Seventeen shallow-draft gunboats had towed the crowded launches shoreward — the 60th Rifles, 2nd Queen's, 15th Punjabis, artillery and rockets, the First Division's 2nd Brigade — anxious to set foot ashore before the French contingent on their starboard quarter. Who invited the bleedin' French, anyway?

There were no trees or grass on the nearing shoreline, only depressing mudflats, glinting in the sun and occasionally stippled by salsola and straggling weed. They could see a few scattered houses, the merest hovels, mud-walled and thatched, but no movement. Behind them *Actaeon*, *Coromandel*, *Cruiser* and *Algerine* followed, cleared for action, their officers searching with glasses the walls of the distant Pehtang forts. There was still no movement. 'Like takin' cake orf a blind baby,' Dando opined, morosely, for the fourth time. He shouldn't have volunteered to accompany the griffins of the 2nd Battalion, the untried men from England — but what could a man do when faced with a return to London, the hopelessness of a discharged soldier, unemployment, the bitter winters —

'Shure,' said Holloran, 'an' ye kin say thet when ye see a bloddy howitzer pokin' up ye' nose.' They could see the town of Pehtang plainly, with the forts on both sides of the river — long, low mounds and castellated walls, as clay-coloured as the surrounding terrain, girdled by ditches. Built at the very edge of firm ground, any assault from the southward, through the deep, tenacious mud, could be shot to pieces by the most leisurely of defences.

The panting steam-gunboat swung to port and the following launch heeled, then grounded. An inch of filthy water washed over their feet, and several sailors were over the side with tattooed arms straining, but the craft was fast. There still remained a half mile of yellow water through which to wade before even the mud was reached, and the bleedin' French were going to be ashore first, sod 'em —

Dando swore as his feet sank into the ooze, with the cloying water rising to his knees. This was what came of volunteering. He must have been soddin' *ghazi*.

Don't volunteer fer nothin', Tom Brownlow would have said. Tom Brownlow, his old rear-rank man, whom Dando had buried on Delhi Ridge after they'd knocked ten kinds of shit out of the Pandies. Don't volunteer fer nothin' — least of all the Queen's bleedin' shilling. Meerut, the Hindun crossing, Delhi. Them was enough for any man's lifetime, wasn't it? He should have taken his discharge. A donkey-cart was the thing. A donkey-cart, and pineapples, bought for tenpence in Covent Garden and sold for a penny a slice, and likely oranges. They kept well. Sod the bleedin' Army.

To the northward the French infantrymen, in their blue coats, red caps and trousers, had already reached firm ground, cheering, and were raising a Tricolour on a pole. Who invited the bleedin' French? Lieutenant Shaw, wading in the van of the 60th, urged his men on angrily. 'Goddammit! You're blasted Riflemen, aren't you? Damn ye' hides! Run!'

'Run, is it?' Holloran spat. To even drag feet through the clinging mud was exhausting — and the Frenchmen had barely got their boots wet. 'Wid ye no prefer us ter fly loik the angels, ye' Honour, sorr? Shure, an' I kin hardly hould me wings from flappin'.' The Lieutenant heard, and bridled, but he made no comment. He was a 'griffin', from England, and he knew better than to embroil himself with these iron-hard, callous 1st Battalion men, who made him feel like a pimple-faced ensign every time he met their musing eyes. Why, in damnation, did the 2nd Battalion need to be stiffened with these insubordinate Indian yallers?

They reached the mud and plunged on, climbing at last to the long spit of firmer ground where the tomb-mounds were — still damp and yielding underfoot, and eroded by reedy creeks and ditches, but with a scattering of bleached grass and scrub. Northward was the miserable clutter of Pehtang and, across their front, a causeway ran southward from the town, fringed with joss poles. Grouped at a low bridge, a mile beyond yet further mud, were horsemen.

The officers' glasses were out, but it was difficult to distinguish much. 'They look like Rykoff's damn' Cossacks,' someone suggested, implying a knowledge of Balaclava. The objects of their interest were mounted on small, shaggy ponies, long-stirruped, and carried lances, round shields, and slung muskets. Numbering some two hundred, they showed no inclination to advance, even had this been easily possible across the mudflats, but watched in silence the British and French regiments milling in disorder as they clambered from the shore.

'Tartars,' someone else said.

'Tartars — that's Chinese fer cavalry,' Dando informed Holloran. He shaded his eyes. The smooth-bore nine-pounders of the Royal Artillery were still hub-deep in mud, and their blaspheming crews would not get them ashore and cleaned of filth for several hours, by which time it would be almost dark. 'Them new Armstrongs, now. Them's the things. They'd knock them bleedin' Tartars orf as easy as spit.' The two batteries of rifled, breech loading twelve-pounders had been the subject of constant speculation. Tested only briefly in India, they had yet to prove that they offered any advantages over the centuries-established muzzle-loaders, with which British artillerymen had attained a high standard of efficiency. The experts were split in their opinions, many sceptical after years of experiment and failure, of breech screws that leaked and vent pieces that exploded. 'Breech loading guns,' protested one investigating committee, 'are far inferior to muzzle-loaders as regards simplicity of construction, and cannot be compared to them in efficiency for active service.' There were similar misgivings in the United States, Prussia, France, and observers would be awaiting with interest the first real baptism of the new Armstrongs — at this moment still lying impotently in the holds of the *Queen of the East*, anchored in the Gulf of Pechihli.

The 60th were jostling into some semblance of order, and it was beginning to rain. Seaward, the red-coated 2nd, mud-spattered and cursing, were spilling out of the filth-encrusted water, behind them the Punjabis in khaki drill, turbans, and equipment and pouches of untanned leather. In the pervading wetness there was nowhere for men to sit or kneel, to place down a rifle. They moved in an untidy column of threes towards Pehtang, through the drizzle, until brought to a halt by a wide ditch which, by the stench that met them, carried the drainings of the town. On the causeway, the Tartar horsemen had turned away and vanished into the dusk, southward.

They waited, soaked and cold. There was no fuel for fires, and the boats had not yet brought ashore the clumsy bell tents into each of which must be crammed twelve or fourteen men. They had nothing save the damp blankets carried in a roll over their haversacks, they were foul with mud, and growing increasingly thirsty, having had nothing but salt rations and the water carried in their canteens since leaving shipboard. For certain, there would be no tents or fresh water tonight. The boats had returned to the Fleet, and there were more urgent commodities than tents and water to be transferred — guns, charges, horses, fodder, staff officers' baggage, and the correspondent of *The Times*. A few hundred yards away the French ridge tents were going up in scores — the famous *tentes à abri*, of which every soldier carried a third section. Shivering and dispirited, the British and Indian infantrymen huddled in groups or walked incessantly among the wet grave-mounds, waiting for dawn. Christ, this was the same as Calamita Bay, the same as the Crimea. Hadn't the soddin' commissariat learned anything since the bleedin' Crimea?

'If ye hed a bucket o' wather, Dando me jewel,' suggested Holloran, 'shure, ye might git a poun' a glass fer it.' They'd known Sergeant Garvin since Chatham, when they had been stumbling recruits and he a barrack-room corporal. A great deal had happened since then, and there existed between the Indian 'yallers' a tolerant relationship, almost intimacy, that annoyed men like Shaw because of its exclusiveness, its implied disdain for others of less experience. Garvin stood over them now.

'Yer can stow yer gab, you two, an' git orf yer lazy arses. Find Moss Rose an' Bathurst, an' don't shout yer mouths orf. Rifles an' side-arms only. Load ball, an' then report ter the Lieutenant.'

They climbed to their feet. 'Wot's it orl about, Sar'nt?'

'We're goin' into Pehtang, quiet-like, wi' Mr Parkes, the Commissioner from Canton.' He added, 'It's likely ye'll have a chance ter fill yer canteens wi' fresh water.'

'Or somethin',' Dando nodded.

'God bless ye, Sergeant, darlint —'

Garvin sniffed. 'Yer can bleedin' watch it. I'm comin' with yer, and so's Captain Williams, o' the Royals.' He paused. 'He was at Inkerman, an' detests the French — so don't be surprised if he expects yer to capture the Pehtang forts ternight, while the Frenchmen are still asleep in their pretty little tents.'

'Christ,' Dando said. 'Yer sure yer need four of us, Sar'nt?'

A minute later the four muddied riflemen stood with shouldered weapons before Lieutenant Shaw. The Sergeant saluted. 'Picquet fer Mr Parkes, sir. Ball loaded an' ready ter march.'

'Ye-es.' Shaw plucked at his lower lip as he eyed the teak-tanned faces before him. Somewhere among this teeming chaos was a coolie with his valise, which in turn contained dry clothing and boots, a flask of brandy and a cold chicken. He'd seen neither coolie nor valise since leaving the deck of the *Alfred*, and he was beginning to think he never would. For a sovereign the damn' heathen had deserted with his second-best green regimentals in which he'd intended to enter Pehtang tomorrow. And the brandy. Goddammit.

'I see,' he said casually, 'that they're all 1st Battalion men, Sergeant.' He would have been incredulous if Garvin had, even for a moment, considered an alternative.

The Sergeant's face was expressionless. 'The Captain did say "an experienced picquet", sir.'

Shaw grunted, then scanned the four riflemen again. 'Holloran, Dando, Rose and Bathurst, eh? I suppose "experienced" is one way of describing them.' He placed his hands behind his back, then smiled coldly. 'When the Chinese take prisoners, they cut off their heads with damn' great swords. Despite my loyalty to Her Gracious Majesty, Queen Victoria, and my untiring devotion to the Regiment, it is my fervent hope that Pehtang is crawling with enemy Chinese, armed to the teeth. With one stroke — or probably four? — the incidence of insubordination, drunkenness and brawling in the 60th Rifles will be all but eliminated.' He glanced at Garvin. 'Carry on, Sergeant.'

Mr Harry Smith Parkes, Commissioner of the treaty port of Canton, was boyishly young, fair-haired and stocky, clad in the generally favoured attire of the Englishman in Africa and the East — a felt helmet with puggaree, tweed Norfolk jacket, moleskin breeches and jackboots. Captain Williams was almost a head taller, in scarlet tunic and tartan trews mired to the knees. 'All Delhi men, Sergeant?'

'Yessir.'

'Good. This is no time for Bagshot Heath soldiers.' Williams turned to the riflemen. 'Now listen, because I'm only telling you once. Since we've landed on this Godforsaken coast we've seen nothing except a squadron of rag-bag Tartars. More important, they've seen us — although, b'God, they could hardly be blind to a hundred and fifty ships anchored off their river. Tomorrow the 2nd Brigade moves on Pehtang, and then the forts. The town's probably abandoned, but the forts could be fully manned and waiting to tear us to shreds. That's what we're going to find out. It's intelligence we want, not a blaze of glory.'

Mr Parkes seemed uncomfortably conscious of his shining new belt and holster. He grinned. 'It's informers we want, chaps, but as politely as possible. We don't want to alarm the Chinese civil. They're only acquainted with their own troops, and they detest 'em. A Chinese army on the march is like a horde of damn' locusts — looting, raping — and they probably think we're the same.' He paused. 'Which, of course, we're not.'

'Don't ye be worryin', yer honour,' offered Holloran. 'Shure, an' we'll be soft an' aisy. Ye cudn't pick four bhoys wid more exparience wid *informers*. If ye'd seen Dando in Meerut, ye'd hev been struck dumb wi' admeerashun —'

'It weren't nuthin' reely,' Dando confessed modestly. 'A quick butt in the gut fer a start. There ain't many blacks as can stand a quick butt in the gut, see? After that, it's orl a matter o' *knowing yer man*. Muslims, now, can't stand pork — so if yer stuff a pig's giblets down 'is throat —'

'Faith,' added Holloran, 'did ye niver hear o' the time when Brownlow an' Dando tuk the Holy Man behin' the guard tent?' He lifted ecstatic eyes. 'Spittin' purple wi' rage, so he wuz, loik an unstrapped lunatic. Jes' make him talk, sez Lieutenant Heathcote, an' there's a double ration o' rum fer yer. Shure, an' the Divil hisself an' all his angels cud niver hev twisted the truth frum thet heathen wid only a rifle sling an' the toe ev a boot.'

''Indoos, now,' Dando said thoughtfully, 'them's different. They don't like bits bein' *cut orf*, becorse after *trans-migrashun* they don't git the bits back, see —'

'Good God,' breathed Mr Parkes.

'Stow it, you two,' Garvin growled. Give these incorrigibles an inch of rope, and they'd hang a bleedin' battalion. But what, sod it, did this dapper little Parkes expect? Likely he'd never had the handling of mutinous Pandies after seeing the defiled and butchered corpses of women, and infants hung on spikes, nor had the task of questioning an insolent Pathan after a missing comrade had been found staked out in the sun, flayed, castrated and blinded. That's when men like Dando and Holloran got information, fast, and an experienced officer lit a cheroot and took a brief stroll, leaving them to it.

And Captain Williams shared the Sergeant's opinion, which was why he had asked for four Indian 'yallers' who knew what they were about — better, even, than his own Crimea men, b'God. There was a recognised code of conduct between civilised armies. Dammit, didn't Lord Raglan refuse to listen to information provided by spies, because it was ungentlemanly? But when you were fighting uncouth savages who tortured and executed prisoners, and couldn't understand English unless it was shouted at them slowly, then it was different. He would have preferred to be without this man Parkes, who promised to be a hindrance, but Parkes was one of the few men accompanying the Army who understood Chinese.

'We'd better get started, Mr Parkes,' Williams suggested. 'We've a long tramp, and the going's hard.' He glanced at the riflemen. 'Single file, no talking, and there's four dozen for anyone who fires without an order.'

They circled the French tents, the glutinous mud sucking noisily at their boots. A troop of dragoons could hardly have destroyed the quietness of the night more effectively. They reached the bridge, where the Tartar horsemen had halted earlier, but the greasy, uneven causeway was now deserted. Their boots and lower legs were sodden and cold. Behind them they could see the lights of the Fleet in the dark void beyond the mudflats — speck-lines of portholes, masthead lights, and red sparks erupting from the funnel of an invisible steam pinnace as it wallowed across the bay. From one of the nearer ships they could hear, faintly, the music of a band. There didn't seem to be any bleedin' sense in not talking.

'Wid all this mud between ye' toes,' said Holloran, 'bedad, it reminds me o' diggin' praties in Donegal, so it does.' He paused. 'Did I ever tell ye, me ol' Dando, ev the time I het the bloddy gombeen man wid the stew-pot?'

*

If it hadn't been for the gombeen man, he would never have gone for the Queen's shilling, never have sweated and fought in India for seven years, nor come to this reeking bog called China. No, that wasn't right. Sure, he might have. The first chilling days of every winter brought hundreds of threadbare and hungry Irish Jackeens to the colours, in Dublin, Derry, Inniskilling, Cork. So far as Patrick Holloran was concerned, the gombeen man probably only precipitated matters.

Those Donegal years were hard. He'd never known boots to his feet and seldom a day when he had a full belly. Two acres of soggy soil, put to potatoes, made a thin return for five people — his parents, himself, and two younger boys. The rent was always in arrears, with the agent threatening eviction from the single-roomed, earth-floored hovel, three miles from Letterkenny. And the winters were cruel, so they were. By the beginning of October, when all vegetables and other gleanings had been eaten, there remained only potatoes, and if the potato harvest had been poor, starvation began. There was nothing to do but wait, to crouch at the hearth with the peat-smoke stinging the eyes, while his father cursed the weather, the landlord, the price of seed, and the black luck of a man with a wife and three children, and never the price of a drop of the stuff to keep the cold from his throat.

Looking back, Patrick Holloran did not recall that his father made any strenuous efforts to improve his lot and, with three boys growing, did progressively less work on the smallholding. Patrick, at sixteen, did not consider it disastrous when his embittered parent walked out of the house one morning, never to return. The greater loss was that of fourteen shillings rent money, which his father took with him. It had been hard enough to accumulate, and would be impossible to replace.

Mrs Mary Holloran, in her mid-thirties, still retained the slim shapeliness and traces of the gentle beauty she had brought with her from County Mayo eighteen years earlier, to marry a handsome Phadrig that only the matchmaker had seen, to a damp bed for Himself and Herself and, later, a second for the boys. She had, too, a streak of Celtic stubbornness, and work-worn hands accustomed to digging and hoeing, scrubbing and mending. But first there was the fourteen shillings. Without the fourteen shillings, she'd never achieve the quarter's rent, which meant eviction and a 'scalp' — a section of roadside ditch roofed with sticks and turf. For the first time in her life she went to the gombeen man — the money-lender — in nearby Letterkenny.

Letterkenny was a single, muddy street of shabby houses, at one end Smyley's Bar, where the jaunting car from Londonderry halted to leave the post, at the other the white-washed Station House, occupied by a sergeant and two men of the Royal Irish Constabulary, visited by the Inspector from Strabane weekly. Roughly midway was the house of Michael Mc'Doon, and Mary Holloran thanked a lead-coloured heaven for the teeming rain that kept the street empty of curious bystanders, for the black shame of it.

Michael Mc'Doon, whom the Devil himself could have taught nothing, was sceptical. Thin as a rake handle, so he was, with eyes that stripped the shift from a decent woman and measured her speculatively.

'Fourteen shillins, is it, Mrs Holloran? And ye've ter foind another thirty-six by quarter day? Shure, an' how are ye supposin' ter pay it back?' He shrugged. 'I've heered that ye' man's up an' left ye. The railway cuttin' in England, I'm guessin'. Ye'll not get a penny piece from a man thet's gone ter the loiks o' London an' Liverpool, so ye'll not. They're tellin' me there's contractors meetin' the boat, offerin' Irishmen twenty-five shillin' a week, an' there's wimmin waitin' ter take the arm ev a man as soon as he's signed.' He leaned forward. 'It's a mortal amount o' money fer a woman, Mrs Holloran, wid the interest. Hev ye any *securitay*?'

'There's the furniture —'

He snorted. 'Shure, an' I kin guess — a few rotten sticks thet wouldn't make a dacent bonfire.' He shook his head.

She tried again. 'Patrick's sixteen, an' big as a man. He kin earn tenpence a day on the road-building at Strabane —'

Mc'Doon raised his eyebrows. 'There's hunnerds o' grown men bein' torned away every day, Mrs Holloran. D'ye suppose they'll hev a sixteen-year bhoy thet has ter walk twelve miles before he picks up a spade?'

Mary Holloran was silent, examining the toes of her dusty feet. Mc'Doon went on. 'Thet houldin' ev yez is hardly enough ter keep the four ev ye, an' ye'll niver raise the rrent. The agent wid be better plased wid two acres o' grazin' then ye' fifty shillin'.'

That meant eviction, and the cottage 'tumbled'. She had seen it happen to others, and the prospect was shuddering. The agent and several constables, with a party of 'crowbar men', would arrive at dawn. The few cottage furnishings would be thrown unceremoniously into the mud of the field, and then the house would be demolished before the eyes of its erstwhile, shivering tenants. There was nothing, then, but to take to the road, crouching in 'scalps' and makeshift shelters, from which local authorities drove them like rats. In summer a tenuous existence might be maintained from roots and berries, filched potatoes and turnips, with the hand of every farmer, land-owner and smallholder against them. Winter meant starvation, with the children's bellies swelling, eyes hollowing, then bronchitis, pneumonia, and cold, stiff corpses to bury, with no priest willing to dirty his feet to plead for the soul of an unworthy scalpeen.

'Aye,' Mc'Doon nodded slowly. 'The winters kin be murderous cauld.' He drummed his fingers softly on the table. 'An' all fer fifty shillin' ter see yez through ter next harvest.'

Mary Holloran raised her eyes. 'Mother ev Mercy —' she began, but Mc'Doon held up a finger. 'Ye'll understand, Mrs Holloran,' he smiled, 'it's one thing borrowin' the money, an' another thing payin' it back wid interest.'

Mary was unwilling to calculate beyond the immediate problem. 'Holy Mother, it'll be paid. Ye kin take my wurd fer it. As I was tellin' ye, wid Himself gone, and Patrick workin' —'

'Shure, an' ye cottiers are all the same, Mrs Holloran — full wid promises an' ol' blarney, an' niver a tinker's rag o' *securitay*, or a hope in Hell o' repayin' ye' borrowin'.' He leaned back in his chair. 'Wud it not be better, Mrs Holloran, if ye offered somethin' else — somethin' that wud cost ye nothin'?'

She met his musing gaze. Something that would cost her nothing? She thought of the two undersized goats tethered behind the cottage, and the meagre pint of milk that each provided daily. There was the rusty black winsey dress that she'd had for seven years, and the little plaster Madonna with the chipped feet that she'd brought from Kilmaine as a bride —

Mc'Doon placed the tips of his fingers together. His smile was fixed, showing tobacco-stained teeth. 'Ye're a handsome woman, Mrs Holloran, an' wid no man ter pay ye the attention ye deserve. Well, now, there's *securitay* fer ye, that I'd be willin' ter consider. Are ye understandin'?' He nodded at a closed door. 'There's a few others in Letterkenny, that I'll not be namin', who pay their borrowin' wid an hour in the little room.'

Mary Holloran felt the blood rise into her face. For eighteen years she had shared a bed with Phadrig Holloran, and the possibility that she might one day surrender her secret body to the hands of another man had never entered her thoughts. She sat rigidly, feeling her heart pounding and her cheeks hot. Mc'Doon rose from his chair, humming.

'It'll be aisy, an' not a soul knowin', 'ceptin' you an' me.' He had moved quietly behind her, and she shivered as his hands slid from her shoulders, entering the top of her bodice. None but her husband's hands had touched her before. Her mouth dried, and Mc'Doon laughed softly. 'Shure, it'll be aisy, an' ye'll be missin' ye' husband —'

The chair spun, crashing to the floor as she tore herself to her feet. 'Aisy, is it? Ye black-hearted desarter from the graveyard! Ye suppose I'd be lettin' ye dirrty me — a married woman wid three sons an' as foin a husband as ever walked? Aisy, ye say?' She pursed her lips and spat, and Mc'Doon recoiled. 'Kape out ev me way, Mc'Doon — or the whole arrmy ev heavenly saints'll not stop me from murrder —!' She whirled, and the door slammed behind her.

She stood in the street, trembling, with the lashing rain soaking into her thin shift and streaming from her hair. The sky was charcoal-coloured over the Derryveagh Mountains, and the road, she knew, would be a morass. In the cottage, three miles distant, the wet would be rising through the sacking-strewn earth floor, and she hoped that one of the boys would have the wit to bring the goats in from the weather.

The boys would be watching the road for her return, waiting to eat. And she had nothing. The bacon knucklebone had already been boiled twice, and would likely turn to glue next time. There were a few pounds of potatoes, the remnants from last year, which stank from damp badness. After today there was tomorrow, and next week. Neither she nor the boys had tasted butcher's meat for almost twelve months. 'Glory be ter Christmas,' Patrick had said wistfully, 'the day we get the mate!'

Mc'Doon was right. It would be easy, and nobody need know. If Phadrig Holloran had deserted her, then he had forfeited a husband's claims, hadn't he? She was entitled to decide for herself. An hour in the little room, was it? How many times for fifty shillings — or say three pounds? In Dublin's Sackville Street a woman could be had for a shilling, against a wall, or eighteen pence on a crumpled bed in a whore-shop. She, Mary Holloran, must be worth more than that? And she could clench her eyes, pretending it wasn't happening.

She turned, retracing her steps to the house of Michael Mc'Doon.

*

'He was a black-hearted Sheeny bastard, was Mc'Doon,' said Holloran. 'He shud hev been hanged from the roof o' Green Street Court-house, so he shud.' They had halted, with the dark and silent confusion of Pehtang beyond an open, castellated gate, a hundred yards ahead. Captain Williams, Mr Parkes and the Sergeant had tiptoed on, while the riflemen waited in the shadows, wiping the wetness from their rifles.

'When my time's expired,' decided Dando, 'I'm goin' ter buy a bleedin' Enfield.'

Holloran paused in the wiping of his weapon. 'And why wid ye be wantin' an Enfield, bedad?'

'I'm goin' ter 'ang it on the bleedin' wall, see?' Dando explained. 'An' every mornin' an' night I'm goin' ter say ter it, "Rust, yer bastard — RUST!"'

'I'll rust yer, wi' a week o' soddin' pack-drill,' said the Sergeant's voice from the darkness. 'Come on, quiet. We're goin' in.'

*

Patrick Holloran, at sixteen, had never known the full truth of it — no more than that his mother had somehow achieved a loan from the gombeen man to pay the quarter's rent. His mild curiosity towards her weekly visits to Letterkenny was not sustained, particularly when she returned with something for the pot — on one glorious occasion a slab of the cheap American bacon that Irish farmers were cursing. Mary Holloran slept alone in the narrow bed behind the blanket, which she had once shared with Himself, while Patrick and his brothers laid head to toe in the other. With the first grey of dawn, Mary Holloran pulled her grubby shift over her shoulders and knelt to blow life into the embers in the hearth, then roused a groaning Patrick for his long tramp to Strabane. He must present himself outside the Presbyterian Church by six, when the roadworks foreman chose a score of men from the two hundred unemployed who shouted, jostled and fought each other with fists to improve their chances of working thirteen hours for tenpence. Patrick had been chosen only once, but torrential rain had halted work before noon, and he had been paid off with fourpence.

The terrible years of 1846 and 1847, when the potato crop had failed, and Ireland had lost a million people by starvation and emigration, had dealt less harshly with the Hollorans and their neighbours. They had watched the straggling groups of destitute, with their pathetic bundles, tramping miserably eastward, towards Londonderry or Belfast, from where government-chartered ships transported emigrants to Quebec for £12 per head, the fare to cover a pound of porridge stirabout and three quarts of water daily. Thousands of them had reached no further than Quebec; they had been disembarked dead, or died within weeks, of malnutrition, typhoid or dysentery. The Hollorans had been hungry, but they had survived, and had remained.

They had survived, that was, until now. Elsewhere, the wounds of the famine years were beginning to heal. There was talk of tenants' rights, or possibly an Act of Parliament to safeguard a cottier's security of tenure, and of vast roadbuilding programmes to provide work. The wheel of ill fortune, however, which had hitherto been relatively charitable to the Hollorans, had not ceased turning.

The two acres' harvest of potatoes had been good. Mary Holloran and the three boys had prised the tubers free of the soggy soil and laid them to dry whilst Patrick dug the long trench in which, straw-protected, the crop would be stored. He had mused, as he dug, that it might be possible this year to buy a young pig, to be fattened in the cottage. It was customary to board 'the gentleman who paid the rrent' in company with the 'Christians', and a hundred-pound pig might fetch thirty shillings in 'Derry —

And he had thought, as he shovelled the potatoes into the trench, that they inclined to softness, but had not been unduly concerned. If they had a pig, now — and perhaps a dozen hens —

Three weeks later the trench, with its full year's harvest, was a viscous, yellow mass of putrefaction. The stench flooded the cottage, fifty yards away.

*

The stink of Pehtang met their nostrils as soon as they passed beyond the black shadows of the gate, with sword-bayonets fixed and the wary, slow pace of men who had done this a hundred times, from Benares to Aligarh, tensed like steel springs to whirl, crash to one knee, cock and fire in the space of a second. It was a costly experience gained during the Mutiny months — a man learned quickly or he never learned at all — but the 60th Rifles had earned from their Sepoy enemies the title of *Shaitan-ke-Pultan*, the Regiment from Hell. Watching the riflemen as they moved from shadow to shadow, Captain Williams was glad that he had resisted the temptation to employ a detachment from his own regiment, the Royals, which would probably have marched into Pehtang with crashing boots and shouted orders, in the manner of Inkerman.

Pehtang was a maze of squalid, narrow streets; in the middle of each was an open gully that carried the communal filth. The houses were decrepit hovels, most with roofs of thatch from which the mud that bound them dripped continuously to the ground under the drizzling rain. Overhead, soaked and tattered awnings hung crazily across the streets, creating murky caverns and obscuring foot-tangling stepways, pot-holes and refuse. Once they froze, and four cap-locks clucked, as an awning, caught by the wind, snapped like a pistol shot, but they saw nothing except a white, skeletal dog who stared at them, barked, then vanished into the gloom with tail between legs.

Pehtang was abandoned or, if any Chinese remained, they had stayed hidden and silent when the Rifles' picquet passed. They reached a wicket fence, and then a rickety wooden bridge across a wide fosse, the depth of which was lost in darkness. 'The fort,' said Captain Williams.

'It smells like an explosion in a shit-pit,' observed Dando.

Holloran turned his head, peering into the gloom, and behind him Rose and Bathurst were standing, statue-like, listening. Ahead, in the blackness of the fort's interior, was a noise of running feet, splashing through the mud. Holloran's rifle came to his shoulder,

'Halt! — or I'll fill ye' liver wid lead!'

The splashing footsteps ceased immediately. 'Ye kin come out ev there, me bucko,' Holloran roared, 'on ye' feet wid yer hands up, or feet first in a blanket —!'

'Don't fire,' Mr Parkes said. 'They won't understand English, dammit.' He shouted, sing-song and incomprehensibly. '*Shui*? *Shih Shui*

—?' Then shouted again, '*Lai pa!*' Moments passed, and Captain Williams heaved a breath. 'All right. When I give the order, we'll give 'em a volley — then follow up with steel. You, Sergeant, take two men to the left. The others follow me to the right.' He drew his pistol. 'Ready —?'

'No — wait!' insisted Mr Parkes. As he spoke, four men emerged from the fort, stooped and trotting. Across the bridge, they halted and knelt.

'They're Chinamen, orlright,' opined Dando. 'Yer can tell that jest by lookin' at 'em.'

'Is these *informers*, ye' honour?' asked Holloran. The four men remained bowed, barefoot, with their ragged nankeen clothes draped in sodden, filthy cotton quilts and their pigtailed heads streaming with water. 'Shure,' went on Holloran, 'ef ye'll give us foive minutes ter introduce thim ter our ramrods, sorr, ye'll hev enough *informin*' ter fill a book, so ye will.'

'That won't be necessary.' Parkes turned, speaking again in Chinese, sharply. '*Ch'i lai!*' The four bedraggled men climbed to their feet, nervously eyeing the surrounding riflemen. 'Are these supposed to be soldiers?' asked Williams.

Parkes laughed. 'No, just coolies. Likely they're watchmen, and they're probably expecting to be decapitated.'

'Jasus,' muttered Holloran, 'what's *decapitated*?'

'It's Chinese fer bein' gelded,' advised Dando.

Holloran considered. 'Faith, I thort that was *castrated*.'

'Ah, but decapitatin's worse. They *mashes* 'em between soddin' great bricks.'

After ten minutes of interrogation, unintelligible to the soldiers, Parkes turned from the prisoners.

'Well, you can't expect too much from coolies like these, but it's plain that the Chinese forces have withdrawn to positions based on the Taku forts, southward, under the Tartar commander, San-Ko-Lin-Sin. And Pehtang's not abandoned, as we thought. The people have just gone to earth, waiting to see what we barbarians intend doing — and with their experience of Chinese troops, I don't blame 'em. But San-Ko-Lin-Sin's no fool and he's certain to dispute any advance across the causeway, which is the only practicable route southward.' He smiled smugly. 'And it was a damn' good thing I stopped you charging into the fort, Captain.

The Chinese have left explosive mines, in pits covered with matting and earth, and with some sort of trigger fuse. You'd have enjoyed the distinction of being the first casualties of the campaign.'

'This Sam Collinson's a crafty sod, ain't 'ee?' said Dando.

'Shure,' agreed Holloran, 'loik Manannán ev the Other Worrld.'

They made their way back towards the causeway, taking the four frightened Chinese with them. Mr Parkes wanted to question them more thoroughly, under more congenial conditions than the mud and darkness of the Pehtang fort — and tomorrow the advance parties of the army would need guides. The coolies followed, resigned, but edging away from the sword bayonets that urged them to a shuffling trot. 'D'ye suppose,' Holloran enquired of Dando in a loud voice, 'thet his honour wid axe thim where we moight get a bottle or two o' *bhang*? I'm thet bloddy dry, ef ye slapped me back I'd spray ye wid dust.'

But their iron-shod boots were clattering on the wet stones of the causeway, and they could see, again, the distant lights of the Fleet. Captain Williams had just holstered his pistol, and then, suddenly, drew it again.

'Halt!' he hissed. 'Quiet!'

They froze immediately. From somewhere ahead of them they could hear, distinctly, the chutter of horses' hooves.

'Ours?' asked Parkes.

'The Dragoons don't begin disembarking until dawn,' Williams murmured, 'and Probyn's and Fane's Sikhs in the afternoon. If they're Tartars, we're cut off.' He paused. 'There's no point in letting them get too close before we find out. Will you hail 'em, sir?'

Parkes cupped his hands around his mouth. '*Shui? Hsien shing shih na li lai ti?*'

'Anyone 'oo understands *that*,' observed Dando, 'jest ain't bleedin' 'ooman.'

The reply from the darkness ahead was also scarcely human. It was a screech. 'Ta! Ta! Shai! Shai!' Holloran sniffed. 'Bedad, there's no sich language.'

'Prepare to receive,' Williams said quietly. The riflemen dropped to one knee, cocked and took aim. They could see nothing, but their target must be confined to the narrow causeway before them, and at a thousand yards the .577 calibre minie ball of the Enfield rifle would tear through four inches of pine.

'Ready? FIRE!'

The guns slammed, vomiting flame, and filling the nostrils with caustic powder-smoke. 'Pick the bones out o' that, yer bastards,' spat Dando — his unvarying comment. They were immediately reloading, biting off the tough endpaper of a fresh cartridge, ramming, reversing the cartridge to thrust home the ball, ramming again, then fumbling in pouch for a percussion cap to thumb into the cap-lock. Three volleys a minute, the musketry manual demanded, but four could be achieved by experienced men who moved like unthinking clockwork. Almost simultaneously, the five Enfields rose to their owners' shoulders.

'Hold fire,' ordered Williams. A horse screamed over a medley of men's voices and chopping hooves. 'Likely they were as surprised as we were. They don't know our strength and we don't know theirs. Like Quarry Ravine, at Inkerman.' He grunted. 'Every time we saw grey coats, we charged, hoping to God they'd decide we were stronger, and break. Sometimes they did, and sometimes they didn't. If they didn't —' He paused. 'Are you game?'

'Es game es Comeragh buck-rabbits, sorr,' assured Holloran. 'Jes' ye give the worrd.'

'All right, then,' Williams nodded. 'At the double, and with all the damn' noise you can make. CHARGE!'

They charged, sword-bayonets levelled and howling like imbeciles, feet crashing and slithering. As Holloran would comment later, an 'intire ridgement o' Bismarck's Prussian Guarrd wid hev been hurrtled into the jaws o' Scáthach' by the pell-mell assault of one officer, a sergeant, and four blaspheming riflemen.

The picquet jostled to a halt at the bridge, mouth-slimed and breathless. The causeway was deserted except for a fallen horse, kicking away its last few seconds of life, a trampled hat with an odd, squirrel-tail plume, and two long-barrelled, matchlock muskets with hemp cords so soaked as to render them useless. The noise of hoof-beats was fading into the distance, southward.

'Well, that's that,' Williams panted, relieved. 'If they had any casualties, they've taken 'em off.'

Mr Parkes came up, breathing hard, with the four coolies trailing. Holloran grinned at him. 'Was thim the swarrm o' locusts ye was tellin' ev, ye honour?' he enquired. 'Shure, an' the few ev us cud march clear ter Paykin, whistlin' a jig.'

'I couldn't whistle bleedin' nuthin',' croaked Dando, 'wi' a mouth tastin' like the barrack-sweeper's arse-clout.'

'Ah,' said Parkes, 'I'll grant you that, at first sight, Chinese soldiers as much resemble European troops as a collection of half-drilled louts in petticoats, but they can be damn' dangerous, especially when they're cornered. They're unpredictable. One day they'll run like women at the first shot, and the next they'll fight like tigers. You can never tell.'

*

At the grave-mounds, Lieutenant George Shaw, commanding No. 4 Company of the 60th, was feeling reasonably buoyant. It had stopped raining, and he had found the coolie with his valise. He had spread a groundsheet, and on it placed his bottle of brandy, cold chicken, four bread rolls, and a lighted hurricane lamp. The situation wasn't too bad, all things considered. He eyed his victuals complacently. Foresight was a wonderful thing.

First, however, he would change his breeches. There was an uncomfortable, itching clamminess about his nether limbs that would mar the enjoyment of brandy and cold chicken. He had peeled off the offending garment and was in the process of tugging his second-best greens over his knees when his mouth-watering anticipation was ruined by the sudden appearance of Sergeant Garvin and four filthy riflemen.

Garvin saluted. 'Mr Parkes' picquet, sir, returned an' orl correct. Permission ter dismiss?'

Shaw fumbled with his cod-buttons. 'Ah — the Indian yallers? No doubt you've stormed the forts, captured the Emperor's first minister, and annexed China on behalf of the Crown, eh?' He was decent at last, and rose to his full height. 'In due course, I'll wager, you'll all get medals.' It was a moment he had savoured. 'In your absence we've managed to issue rum and water to all ranks, but we considered that, prancing around Pehtang, you'd be filled to the gills.'

Sergeant Garvin was silent, then, 'Ye mean, sir, that there was no ration kept fer the picquet?'

The Lieutenant shrugged. 'A pity, I'll agree, Sergeant — but nothing much to worry men who fought at Delhi, eh? Didn't I hear someone say they'd sucked pebbles on the march to Baghpat?'

'If there's one thing I 'ate more than screw-gun mules,' Dando spoke from the corner of his mouth, 'it's bleedin' cocky officers.'

The tall figure of Captain Williams suddenly thrust itself into the pool of yellow lamplight. He grinned. 'Shaw, isn't it? I thought I'd dawdle across to tell you that your fellows did damn' well tonight. The General's sending a note to Colonel Palmer, and writing the action into his despatches.'

'I'm glad to hear it, sir,' Shaw offered.

Williams' eyes fell to the groundsheet, and widened. 'You've organised some vittles, eh?' He reached downwards to take up the bottle. 'And brandy, Goddam!' He pursed his lips. 'There's nothing like brandy after a four-hours' tramp in the mud, Shaw — take my word for it. I'll allow you take care of your fellows pretty damn' well in the 60th. It'd never happen in the Royals, b'God —'

'I say, sir —' Shaw protested, but he was too late. The bottle had sailed towards the file of watching riflemen, to be caught expertly by Dando. 'Share it between you,' Williams instructed, 'and quick about it.' Dando was already extracting the cork with his teeth as the Captain turned back to Shaw. 'If you're ever in the Royals' mess, old chap, I'd be delighted to return hospitality, y'know. Any time.' He grinned again, affably, then vanished into the darkness with the riflemen hurriedly following.

'God save ye, Captain darlint,' chortled Holloran. 'May ye' honour's cow niver run dry!'

Alone, Lieutenant Shaw stared blankly at the cold chicken on the groundsheet, then took a running kick at it which sent it hurtling into the gloom. 'Why didn't ye take the bloody lot?' he shouted.

*

Distant by several grave-mounds, Holloran drained the last of the bottle and sighed. 'Faith, thet was a foin drop o' the stuff, so it was. Ye'd not get better at Smyley's Bar in Letterkenny, an' that was brewed by himself. Shure' — he glanced at his companion — 'did I ever tell ye, me ol' Dando —?'

'Of the time yer 'it the bleedin' goblin wi' the stoo-pot?' Dando, with his cap over his eyes, was almost asleep.

'Gombeen man,' Holloran corrected. 'Michael Mc'Doon, the misbegotten scutt ev a Judas. T'ree pence interest in every shillin' — per *wake* — wid ye believe it?'

An interest of threepence in the shilling, per week, was not unusual, and thousands of Irish peasants, faced annually with starvation but with the sublime optimism of Micawber, resorted again and again to the gombeen man, invariably borrowing beyond a capacity to repay, then borrowing again to pay the interest, with all chattels of value long gone, every penny earned and every miserable crop for years ahead owed to the detested gombeen man. The Irish blamed their sick soil, the weather, the rents, the English and, most of all, their black luck, but seldom their own peculiar disinclination to work more than was barely necessary to eat for today. Tomorrow was remote, and next week even more so.

Young Patrick was, however, sufficiently mature to appreciate the dangers of the gombeen man. His mother had, he knew, already achieved a loan, and the only collateral of which he knew was the potato crop. He had previously wondered — but only briefly — how they would live, or even raise subsequent rents, with the potato crop mortgaged. Now, with the crop irretrievably ruined, the question of survival during the coming year had become critical. If rent demands — known as 'gales' — were not met, eviction was certain. Could his mother achieve another loan? Patrick was not in the slightest degree concerned about the consequences of obtaining a further loan which could not be repaid, only with the likelihood of obtaining it. What security, bedad, could his mother offer Michael Mc'Doon now? He was soon to discover.

He had failed yet again to catch the eye of the roadworks foreman at Strabane, but tramping homeward he had seen the fine black cockerel with the red comb — a wanderer from some nearby smallholding — fluttering in a snare intended for rabbit or hare. It had been the work of seconds to turn the bird's neck and thrust the still-struggling trophy under his jacket. Never had he walked so fast, sometimes breaking into a trot, to reach the cottage. Never had the road seemed so long. It was a good thing to bring home, so it was. Would it be roasted tonight, basted with the last of the carefully-conserved bacon fat? And the remains, with the giblets, stewed with an onion and turnip, tomorrow? To be sure, not a scrap would be wasted, and he would watch the hungry anticipation in the younger boys' faces as they sat with their spoons, waiting for the succulent mess to be ladled from the black, iron pot in the hearth. Sure, it was a fine thing to bring home.

Approaching the cottage from the rutted Letterkenny road, he was surprised to see his smaller brothers, barefoot and dirty, seated on a broken hurdle, their attention apparently concentrated on the cottage door. He was surprised that they should be here at all, rather than tramping the area in search of ha'pennyworths of jobbing. It was equally odd that, being here, they should be so innocently engaged. Still, it was not important. Faith, didn't he have the fine cockerel under his coat? And wouldn't the boys be on their feet, and hollerin', when they saw their mother's fingers plucking it ready for the old black pot?

He was laughing as he entered the door and, after the outside sunlight, it was several seconds before his vision adjusted to the damp gloom of the windowless room. Then his laughter died. In his father's chair, at the rickety table, sat Michael Mc'Doon, the gombeen man.

Mc'Doon was as surprised as Patrick. He rose to his feet and, simultaneously, Mary Holloran emerged from behind the ragged blanket that curtained her bed, tugging downwards at her skirt. Her face was flushed.

The moment was not intelligible to Patrick. Indeed, had Mc'Doon been sufficiently astute, he might have masked the reason for his presence with some counterfeit explanation, and left Patrick, if puzzled, unaware of any misdemeanour. The gombeen man, however, chose to be brazen.

'The Divil! Ef it isn't the man himself — wid a pocketful o' money from the road-workin', an' a foin bird thet's niver come out ev Strabane market. Ye'll be gettin' yeself a cutaway an' a red wais'coat fer Sunday Mass, will ye not?' Mary Holloran stood stiffly, silent.

Patrick allowed the cockerel to drop to the floor. His eyes were intent on his mother. "There was no worrk agin today,' he said slowly.

"Ah, the luck ev it,' Mc'Doon sympathised. He drew a hand from a pocket. "Shure, an' here's a penny ter change it fer ye!' The coin clattered on the tabletop, dragging down Patrick's gaze. Already, on the table, lay two sovereigns. Patrick had never held a sovereign in his hand during his whole life.

'Aye,' Mc'Doon sniffed, 'two poun'. Thet's better than tenpence a day thet ye're not gettin', and ye'll not be payin' the rrent wid chickens. But ye' mother'll kape ye from beggin' skilly from the parish —'

Patrick was beginning to understand, and there was bile in his throat. How did a boy of sixteen contend with a situation like this, with his mother saying nothing? Mary Holloran had not moved. 'Ye're a black-mouthed bastard, Mc'Doon,' Patrick said. 'Since me father's not here, I'll smash ye' face meself.'

'And ye'll be in Bishop Street Gaol, I'm tellin' ye,' retorted Mc'Doon, 'wid ten years transportation —' With the table separating him from Patrick, he was totally unprepared for the manner of the other's assault, Patrick stooped to his right, picked up the heavy iron pot from the hearth and, in almost the same movement, hurled it with all his strength at Mc'Doon's head. 'Ten years, is it —?' The vicious missile struck the gombeen man full in the face, shattering teeth and nose. He spun backwards, falling, with hands clamped to a crimson face and retching.

Mary Holloran shrieked. 'Mother ev God —!' She ran forward and fell to her knees. 'Whit hev ye done?'

'Jes' whit I said,' Patrick panted. 'Smashed his face.'

'It's nothin' ter be proud ev, ye shameless, ungrateful blackguard! It's a cruel thing ter do ter a Christian thet's kept ye fed, an' paid the rrent, since the day Phadrig Holloran desarted ye —'

*

With his back against the grave-mound, Rifleman Holloran sucked meditatively on his pipe. 'Shure,' he mused, 'wimmin's quare, so they are. Ter think ev it! I moight hev got mesself ten years' transportation, growin' praties an' milkin' goats in New Sout' Wales. Instead, faith, I tuk the Quane's bloddy shillin' in Inniskillin', fer ten years ev punishment drills an' rig'lations an' bloddy colour-sergeants, murtherin' Paythans an' salt beef. Thet's luck fer ye.'

His pipe-bowl, cupped in his hand, glowed red. 'Did I ever tell ye, Dando me jewel —?' But Dando was already asleep.

4

General San-Ko-Lin-Sin, in Tung-ku, was uncertain. The *Soldier's Manual* to which he had given careful study, said nothing in all its eighteen chapters about fighting barbarians. It said, indeed, very little about fighting at all. There were interesting passages covering modes of marching, building bridges, military music, exhortations on bravery, and threats of punishment and death in the event of cowardice. The *luh-ying*, the Chinese army, had little experience of campaigning against European troops. True, the British and French had received bloody noses during the glorious victory of Taku, last year, but they had returned, strongly reinforced, and were already ashore — 30,000, it was reported, including a labour corps of 2,500 coolies. They must not advance further, ordered a decree from the Great Council of Peking. The *fan-kwei*, the foreign devils, must be cut to pieces by the invincible Tartar cavalry on the plain before Sinho. In the unlikely event of any of them surviving beyond Sinho, then they must be massacred by the forts of Taku.

Fortunately, the General had accumulated a great deal of information about the Europeans. Many of the Chinese clerks employed in Hong Kong and the treaty ports spoke and read English, and it was not difficult to compel intelligence from them by either threats or bribes. The English, in particular, had numerous uncivilised habits. They had been seen, for instance, to kiss their women in public. They passed things with one hand, opened a gift in the presence of the giver, ate with kitchen utensils instead of chopsticks, and mixed milk and sugar with their tea. They consumed raw beef, rotten pheasant, and nauseating foods like cow-milk cheese and kippers. Finally, they bathed so often because they smelled so much.

Such contemptible people would surely know little of the art of war. Indeed, one Peking official had suggested that there was no need for fighting. It was only necessary for China to threaten to terminate the trade in tea and rhubarb, and the barbarians would capitulate.

Of his own forces, San-Ko-Lin-Sin was confident. The infantry were equipped with iron, smooth-bore, matchlock muskets, with a match of hemp or coir. It was true that the weapons were almost useless in wet or windy weather, but the General did not intend to fight in the rain. Chinese soldiers wore loose jackets of brown or yellow, with blue trousers, and a cuirass, or surcoat, of quilted and doubled cotton cloth. The back of the surcoat bore the word *yung*, meaning courage, and the breast was painted with the symbol of the service to which the soldier was attached — the governor's, the commandant's, or the Emperor s.

The Chinese cavalry was drawn mainly from the Tartar tribes and, as such, was particularly disliked by the peasantry. Mounted on small, Mongolian horses, with a wooden saddle, large circular-soled stirrups, and a single rein, cavalrymen carried musket, sword, lance, and a round, rattan shield. They were excellent horsemen, and their animals wiry and quick — far more than a match, the General decided, for the slow-plodding, heavy horses that the barbarians were landing in the Gulf of Pechihli.

It was his artillery that caused San-Ko-Lin-Sin most concern. The guns were of a confused miscellany of type and calibre, so that a fort mounting thirty guns was unlikely to have two alike. Some were Chinese-cast, others European. All were antique, and the quality of black powder varied widely. The most effective type was the gingall, mounted on a tripod — a long-barrelled gun, from six to fourteen feet, and firing a ball weighing from 4 ounces to one pound. In the field, the gingall barrel was carried by one horse and the tripod by a second.

The European barbarians scoffed that Chinese soldiers were trained to miss a man at twenty paces. They did not remember that the Chinese were using gunpowder during the Han dynasty, when all Europeans were cavemen.

The Tartar vedettes were daily reporting the foreigners' activities in and around Pehtang, and it was plain that they were preparing for an advance across the causeway towards Sinho, the Taku forts, and the road to Peking. There had already been several skirmishes, involving exchanges of shots, but from which no military conclusions could be drawn. Then, however, the Tartars had brought in the twenty prisoners.

Of the twenty, sixteen were Cantonese coolies, and of no account. The others consisted of an Irish sergeant of the 44th Regiment, a Scottish private of the 3rd Buffs, and two Madrassi sappers. The party had apparently taken a wrong road, and the two Europeans, at least, were hopelessly drunk when the Tartars came upon them — or, as the Chinese described it, suffering from 'Samshu pigeon'.

By the time the captives reached the quarters of San-Ko-Lin-Sin they had been roughly handled, and the two Europeans had regained their sobriety. They had also regained a degree of truculence, and when ordered to kowtow before the General, both refused. San-Ko-Lin-Sin was surprised at this display of discourtesy, but attributed it to the ill-breeding common to all foreigners. He instructed his interpreter to repeat the order, adding that a second refusal would mean death. The sergeant, who could recall nothing about kowtowing in Queen's Regulations, decided to kneel, but the belligerent Scot stood firm and, for good measure, mouthed a torrent of vilification that confounded the interpreter. The General was sorry, but insolence had only one reward. The soldier was dragged to the ground and his head hacked off with a sword.

*

Lieutenant General Sir Hope Grant, KCB, was also suffering from uncertainty, although nobody would have guessed so from a manner that was calm and impressive. Grant was an experienced officer, having served with distinction in the Sikh War, and during the Sepoy Revolt, in which he commanded the Cavalry Brigade throughout the Siege of Delhi. Earlier, he had owed his first Staff appointment to his skill as a violoncello player. Lord Saltoun, commanding a brigade in China in 1842, was a violinist, and wished for an accompanist. The musical abilities of Captain Hope Grant, of the 9th Lancers, were recalled, and for no other qualification he was promoted to brigade-major.

Grant, however, had outlived that minor embarrassment; most people had forgotten it. He had since proved himself capable and courageous, and he was popular with all ranks. He was confident in his men, and they in him. What worried him most was the prospect of failure — or even success that was less than overwhelming — against an enemy whom everyone considered to be an undisciplined rabble, to be beaten without effort.

The British Army was not the world's largest, but it was the most professional, and a number of good commanders had emerged from the hard schools of the Crimea, the Persian War, the Indian Mutiny and the North-west Frontier. Competition was keen. The Horse Guards and

Westminster had grown accustomed to success, and Grant knew himself under the shadow of the frustration suffered before the Taku forts during the previous year — although this had followed the impetuosity of the Royal Navy rather than anything of Grant's inspiration. Still, he considered himself on trial, and he had an uncomfortable feeling that the Chinese were going to provide stiffer opposition than anyone envisaged.

He did not care for the Chinese. They bound the feet of the girl children they did not kill, and enslaved their women. They ate such revolting things as unborn mice, monkeys' brains still hot from a hacked-off head, hundred-year-old eggs, snakes cooked alive in boiling rice, sea slugs and bird's nest soup. Chinese wine was comparable to a one-and-sixpenny bottle of South African port with water and treacle added, and Chinese music was execrable.

Grant would also have been happier without his French allies. Lacking the benefit of garrisons in Hong Kong and India, they were desperately short of horses and mules, and made constant demands on the British. French agents in Japan, trying to buy ponies, accused the British of having already skimmed the best from the market, and General de Montauban's continuous insistence on maintaining parity of reputation in all military matters was petty and obstructive. Grant had ordered two British soldiers to be flogged for stealing a pig, but French troops were permitted to pillage and vandalise at will. Bad blood was already developing.

The cattleship *Zouave* had arrived from Chusan, with only 85 oxen alive of the 250 she had embarked ten days earlier. It was not an isolated case, and the commissariat calculated that, between the number of oxen purchased and the number that arrived in a fit state for the butcher, beef was costing twelve shillings per pound — an impossible price.

But the annoying episode of the drunken British captives had made his demands for sterner discipline rather amusing in the eyes of the French. A sergeant and a private, supervising a party of coolies in taking a grog issue from Pehtang to Sir Robert Napier's 2nd Division, had drunk themselves stupid, lost their way, and were taken by a Tartar patrol. Some days later the sergeant, and most of the coolies — deprived of their pigtails — had returned. The sergeant had a colourful story to tell of Private Moyse, who had refused to kowtow before a Chinese mandarin, and had been beheaded for his patriotism. Perhaps hoping to alleviate his own punishment for dereliction of duty, the sergeant also claimed extensive knowledge of Chinese military plans, having overheard his captors discussing them. Asked how he had acquired this knowledge, since he did not understand a single word of Chinese, he could only offer, 'Shure, thim fellows hev no sacrets at orl, sorr.'

Worse, the story was already on its way to *The Times*, in London, where the heroism of a simple soldier, Private Moyse, was to be lauded in verse —

Last night among his fellow roughs
He jested, quaffed and swore,
A drunken private of the Buffs
Who never looked before.
Far Kentish hopfields round him seemed
Like dreams to come and go,
Bright leagues of cherryblossom gleam'd
One sheet of living snow.
Yes, honour calls! with strength like steel
He puts the vision by;
Let dusky Indians, whine and kneel,
An English lad must die.
And thus with eye that would not shrink,
With knee to man unbent,
Unfaltering on its dreadful brink,
To his red grave he went...
So let his name through Europe ring
A man of mean estate,
Who died, as firm as Sparta's king,
Because his soul was great...

Moyse, however, was no Kentish lad. He had been an unprincipled Scot of 32, with a long record of drunkenness and insubordination, and his behaviour before San-Ko-Lin-Sin was more likely his typical reaction towards authority than a conscious act of heroism. Moyse resented any order, from anybody.

5

She was named Yü, meaning Jade, but she had never known who had chosen the name. She knew almost nothing of her birth except that her parents must have been peasants, and poor, for her feet had been left unbound and ugly — an omission that had filled her with shame on many occasions; it lowered her in the eyes of others and severely reduced her desirability as a wife or concubine. Yü had sometimes mused on the cruelty of parents who neglected a girl-child in this way, and many times she had watched, with a pang of envy, the old women newly binding a baby's feet. The arch of each foot was broken and the ball of the large toe forced back against the heel. The four smaller toes were also broken and pulled under the sole, and then the entire foot strapped so tightly as to restrict any further growth. It was important that, when adult, a woman's foot should not measure four inches in length, nor be wider than two.

True, feet-binding was often painful, and many girl-children died from gangrene or other infections, but what was a little pain? And there were many unwanted girl-children. Yü would have given anything — had she anything to give — to possess flower feet.

It was not, as the foreign barbarians assumed, a device to compel upon women a graceful, teetering gait, nor to immobilise them and thus safeguard their chastity, but only to develop a large pad of muscle on the inside of each thigh, which made sexual intercourse more enjoyable for husband or brothel patron. Did not the old proverb say, 'Every flower foot means a jar full of baby's tears'? But a girl-child destined to spend her life toiling in the fields, with her back stooped under heavy burdens, or sweating with mattock and hoe for eighteen hours of every day, was better without bound feet.

Yü remembered situations more easily than the identities of people. She remembered a mud-clogged pond, and geese that strutted with necks angrily outstretched. There had been flat, hedgeless fields, a watermill clanking and splashing, an immense, miniature forest of green millet stalks, with stems like bamboos, into which she crawled and, in the cool shade, watched above her the willowy leaves against the sky rustling in the slightest breeze. She remembered huge, speckled watermelons and copper-coloured pumpkins weltering in black soil, and patient, labouring oxen with a spear-goad swaying over their scimitar horns.

Who had been the man on whose strong shoulders the infant Yü had ridden, chuckling, and pulling at his hair? And where had been the orchards, with trees laden with apples and yellow pears? And the lines of stubby vines, black with the raisinlike grapes that smeared her baby cheeks with carmine?

She knew that these things had all been before the Hunger, and her fragmentary memories of the Hunger had since been supplemented by the stories of older people. It had begun with a bad season because of the lack of rain, and many had gone to the money-lenders, confident that next year would be fruitful and all would be recovered. But next year was worse, and the next. The soil had turned to dust, trees and crops had shrivelled, and animals had died. Precious seed was eaten, bands of hungry, desperate peasants roamed the land, stealing from others who had scarcely more than themselves, and women boiled nettles, berries, and even earth. Poultry, dogs and cats had long disappeared. There were dust-storms, blown from the Gobi and Ordos deserts, with corpses on every road, in every field, with none to bury them. The winters were savage, the houses and barns being progressively pulled down to provide fuel for burning, or for selling in the nearest towns. Lawlessness prevailed, with magistrates fled and law officers turned brigand.

There was still food to be had, at a price. In the far South there was no famine, and from Chekiang, Honan and Anhui, by barge, ship, or caravan escorted by soldiers, travelled flour and rice, dried fish, soy beans and sesame oil, but only the wealthy could afford these things. The peasants scratched for roots and crouched in their hovels, waiting, starving. Infants sucked at milkless breasts, and died. Wolves roamed in packs, hunting the remaining living and tearing at the dead.

She knew, at least, why she had ridden, for the last time, on the man's shoulders. He may have been Yü's father, an uncle, or an older brother; that she could not guess. Nor had she been aware then, as she swayed and laughed, high above the ground, that the man was carrying her to Tien-tsin, to sell her.

Yü was fortunate. Many of the peasants, for several years, had been killing their girl-children. They were useless mouths, to be fed during adolescence and then lost at marriage. Women were chattels, beasts of labour, bearers of children — preferably boy-children — and were permitted to own no property. A man took a woman for wife and her sisters for concubines, or went to the brothel, where there were women in plenty.

Tien-tsin was vast. Yü had never imagined that there could be so many houses and so many people in one place. The river was thronged with junks, sampans, and lorchas. Some of the streets were paved, and houses were built of slate-coloured brick, instead of the mud and straw she had always known, with windows of trellis and varnished paper. The massive gate through which her guardian pushed his way was choked with humans and animals — coolies, malformed and sore-covered beggars, muddy children and heavily-laden women — and there was a deafening, constant noise, of shouts, hoarse trumpets and drums. A camel train had newly arrived from Peking, the beasts tugging their heads from local bullock wagons and their drivers screeching insults. There were many soldiers, armed with muskets and swords, some carrying huge fans or paper umbrellas painted in glaring colours, and at every corner men sat while barbers dressed their pigtails or shaved heads and eyebrows. Kerbside blacksmiths, cobblers and letter-writers, carpenters and mat-makers all added their yells to the general chaos of twirling hand-drums, clappers, gongs and bells. Only foodstuffs seemed lacking, and only a few shops and stalls offered thinly-spread stocks of cabbage leaves, lentils, mussels, occasional dog-meat or, at extortionate prices, dried fish, goat, and plucked pigeons. Even wealthy Tien-tsin had felt the grip of the Hunger.

Yü was doubly fortunate. Her guardian did not take her immediately to a brothel. She was too young, even for those connoisseurs who insisted that untried, immature children were the most piquant, not caring if the little concubines survived the haemorrhage and dirty stitching that followed. Yü was taken to the house of P'u Sung Ling, a mandarin of the fifth class, whose rank was announced to all by the coveted plain glass button sewn to the crown of his hat. But she would not meet P'u Sung Ling yet.

Instead, she was placed on the ground before a short old woman with black, sharp eyes, and a coinlike mole on her chin from which grew, antenna-like, several three-inch hairs. To Yü's amazement, her male companion knelt and placed his forehead to the dust. She had never seen a man kowtow to a woman before.

The woman snorted. 'Hi yah! She has big feet!'

Yü's companion grovelled. 'She is an unworthy child, and unfit for the eyes of men, but she is strong, and will work hard. There is no disease in her, and she will give many years.'

'Tien-tsin is full of unwanted girl-children. Why do you plague me with another? It should be law that every second girl-infant should be killed, for *yin*, the element of darkness and evil, is female. Is it not said that the most beautiful and gifted girl-child is not as desirable as a deformed boy? Pah! And you bring me a girl with big feet!'

'She will work willingly, and eat very little — the waste from your table, a few leaves of cabbage, or a scrap of fish —'

'Fish! Do you know the price of fish, you fool? Do you think I would squander *fish* on this wretch? Why not pork, or fat goose stuffed with chestnuts and shrimps?' She reached forward a clawlike hand to grasp Yü's shoulder. The child was well-fleshed and clean, with a pretty face and good teeth — not like most of the thin, lice-ridden town-reared children. This one, as the man said, would work hard. In a few years, if fed reasonably, she would develop into a comely little piece with good breasts and buttocks. It was a pity about the feet —

A woman without flower feet did not have the fine, strong thighs which were a necessary attribute of the accomplished concubine. Big feet could be hidden, but the ability to please men could not be simulated. This child would never fetch a high price, nor would be likely to attract the attention of a wealthy merchant, a government official, or a magistrate, but there were others — clerks, shopkeepers, undiscerning farmers — who might pay a few cash to have an hour with her.

She sniffed. 'She is worth nothing. Less than nothing. In Tien-tsin she will probably sicken and die. All these country brats do. A fish from a mountain rock pool will not breathe in a city ditch. You cannot expect that I should pay for the privilege of relieving you of a hungry mouth. If you think so, you may take her away and kill her.'

For several moments the man remained silent and unmoving, while Yü stood eyeing her toes, uncomprehending. There were the distant, unreal noises from the market place, of bells and gongs and shouting hawkers, and the sun was hot. The old woman snorted again, impatiently, then drew a hand from a wide sleeve to toss down four or five small coins. The man scrabbled for them gratefully. 'May the five happinesses be yours —' He did not glance again at Yü, and in seconds he had gone.

The old woman watched his departure, then placed her hands back into her sleeves. Yü looked up at her with throat choked. 'All right, child,' the woman nodded. 'He has gone. You can weep now.' Her eyes were less hard, but not pitying, and when Yü made no response she said, 'I am Tien Mu. The house-women call me Mother Lightning, because I punish swiftly.'

*

Yü quickly recognised that there was only one authority in the big house that had any lasting relevance to her — that of Tien Mu — but many weeks passed before she established the old lady's precise place in the household's hierarchy. Mother Lightning was the senior wife of P'u Sung Ling and, as such, dominated all other women in the home of her husband — secondary wives, concubines and menials. There were others who bullied Yü, sometimes beat her, but all submitted, immediately and without question, to the harsh rule of Tien Mu.

It was doubtful if P'u Sung Ling, the master, was even aware of Yü's existence. A mandarin of the fifth class, of the plain glass button, he was a man to be reckoned with in Tien-tsin, and ranked high in the City's administration. He had a handsome litter, painted red with golden storks, carried by four coolies and preceded by musicians, and devoted most of his day to civil matters — street lighting, maintaining the watchmen, the cleansing of community wells, supervising the markets, the transfer of lands. Yü watched him from afar — a nervous little man with a wispy beard and elongated fingernails encased in silver sheaths. He never glanced in her direction as she and her fellows kowtowed, pressing their brows to the floor that she scrubbed daily.

If P'u Sung Ling was a power in Tien-tsin, however, he represented a figure of negligible importance in the great capital of Peking, a hundred miles up the Pei-ho river, where there were numerous 1st and 2nd class mandarins, of the red and flowered-red buttons. And the Emperor, the personal name of whom could never be mentioned by lesser men, but who was referred to as the Son of Heaven, or Lord of Ten Thousand Years. Pu Sung Ling lived, day to day, in constant fear of Peking, of criticism, admonition or, worst of all, the dreaded summons to the Summer Palace. What mattered an unwanted peasant girl-child, with unbound feet, who scrubbed and scoured, cleaned vegetables and plucked poultry, and lived on scraps in a corner of a kitchen that he had never seen?

Yü did not consider herself either ill-treated or overworked. True, from Tien-tsin she could no longer see the distant Heng Shan mountains, over which the setting sun transmuted the whole landscape into glorious hues of purple, silver and rose, the mountain summits crested with fairy palaces and castles of ivory, pagodas of gold, nor could she chase frogs among the marsh-reeds, to feed the clamouring ducks of the green-slimed pond. There were compensations.

During the few years that she remembered she had seldom known better than a daily bowl of bean curd and cabbage. The pigs and poultry were for market, not for eating, and only on rare and special occasions had she tasted meat or fish. In recent months, with the stock dead and the once rich earth turned to impotent, yellow dust, there had been many times when she had sipped at hot water floating with a few sour leaves to keep the hunger from her belly. Now, in the house of P'u Sung Ling, although the scrapings in her bowl were those spurned by the other menials, the sweepers and bath-house women, garden coolies, scullions and chamber-servants, she had a full belly, with often a delicacy that her betters had overlooked — a whole shrimp, a fragment of duck, a fish-head, or the unfamiliar rice that had come from south of the Yangtze. A full belly and bruises were better than hunger and a glorious view of the Heng Shan mountains.

Yü seldom considered her future. It would be decided for her, and there was little or nothing she could do to influence it. The coveted status of wife was unlikely, because of her ugly feet, but she could hope that, in due course, one of the Master's sons would notice her and, despite her impediment, take her to his bed pallet. Any of the sons, that was, except Kiaking, the strange one.

Kiaking was sixteen, moon-faced, with a loose mouth and eyes that, when he was excited, rolled uncontrollably. His speech was slurred and usually childish, and he dragged a leg when he walked. It was whispered that, at his birth, no food had been left at the door to placate the spirits of wicked men, who had left him cursed.

Yü knew exactly what was required of women, and was as completely resigned as all her fellows. Men, between their thighs, had a jade stem, women a flowery path, and when the two were joined, dew dropped into a blooming peony to begin the first year's life of an infant. It was, she anticipated, an experience of the utmost happiness. Except, that was, with Kiaking, the strange one.

The women lived in fear of him. Kiaking waited in quiet places for unsuspecting menials, then opened his clothes to flaunt his genitals, grinning. Cornered by him, there was no escape; he was incredibly strong and sadistically spiteful. What house-woman dared battle with a son of the Master? She could only acquiesce respectfully, numbly. A moment's display of distaste or resistance provoked him to bestiality. It was better to lie still, hoping he would be sated quickly, than be kicked and punched, to have pubic hair wrenched out by his clawing fingers, and be left bleeding and painwracked. But Kiaking had not noticed Yü yet. She was insignificant and unworthy, with ugly feet.

Still, she knew what was expected of her, in time. If she did not have the periodical indulgence of a jade stem she would become sour and ill-tempered. She knew the story of the elderly emperor, who summoned a physician to attend the apparent malady of his entire host of Imperial concubines. The physician's recommendation was that a number of lusty young men be sent to the women's quarters daily, to which the emperor reluctantly agreed. On visiting his concubines a week later, the emperor found them all in glowing health, warm-cheeked and laughing happily, but a group of haggard and emaciated men kowtowed shakily. 'Who are these lame wretches?' enquired the emperor. The concubines giggled coyly, then answered, 'Lord, these are the dregs of the medicine.' If Tien Mu's irascibility was any guide, Yü considered, it was probably a very long time since the senior wife had enjoyed a jade stem.

Yet it was only from old Mother Lightning — Tien Mu — that Kiaking shrank, abashed, when she lashed him with a contemptuous tongue, the long hairs on her chin quivering and her lips drawn back over broken teeth. Her intervention had saved several of her brood of female menials from crippling injury. She called him a bitch-sniffing Korean pig-coolie, who needed to be gelded in the manner of the Lob-nor camels, who had their testicles crushed between heavy stones. Had he heard of the paramour of the First Emperor's mother, whose organ was of such size that he could fit a cartwheel over it, and spin it? Kiaking should find himself a cartwheel, with a large axle-hole, instead of snatching at women who had work to do. Kiaking detested Tien Mu. He might easily have swept the old lady aside with a fling of his arm, and there were occasions when, loose-mouthed with eyes rolling, it seemed that he might do so, but she stood her ground, meeting glare for glare and her rattan switch raised. And Kiaking never defied old Mother Lightning.

6

It was 4 am, and the Allies' advance on Sinho, the first stage towards the Taku forts and the road to Peking had begun. The British 2nd Division and all cavalry, under Sir Robert Napier, were to follow a route across the mudflats, reconnoitred a few days previously by Lieutenant-Colonel Wolseley, to take the flank of the enemy's defence lines, while the 1st Division followed the French along the causeway, directly at the enemy front.

The red-trousered French infantry, with Thouvenin-Minié rifles shouldered, went off at a brisk pace behind a clatter of drums and trumpets which, however, quickly lost enthusiasm and fell silent. The flanking column met trouble almost immediately, with ammunition limbers foundering in the mud, the whipped horses and mules plunging, and gunners, drivers and coolies to their waists in filth, straining at gunwheels. Probyn's and Fane's regiments, and the Dragoon Guards, followed. The cavalry horses were well-groomed, but showed all the signs of a long sea voyage followed by ten days' confinement, fetlock deep in the semi-liquid mud of the Pehtang fort.

'What d'yer bleedin' expect?' asked Dando, who could be relied upon to opinionate authoritatively on most subjects. 'Yer can't expect a soddin' Balaclava if yer feed 'orses on bird-seed an' sewer-water.'

The mud, at least, was something tangible, something that could be contended with, and eventually mastered. Behind them was Pehtang. They had grown heartily sick of Pehtang, with its pervading stench, the open drains, the narrow, pot-holed streets choked with soldiers, coolies, sailors, Sikhs, horses, bullocks, mules and carts, roving parties of Frenchmen armed with shovels and bill-hooks and hunting the black, pot-bellied pigs that ran screeching. There had been a constant fear of cholera, dysentery and typhoid, but amazingly there had been little illness — mainly, Holloran claimed, because he had recited 'the Divil's Mass backwards twoice a day, an' thet's a bloddy pow'ful curse, so 'tis.'

The British on the causeway waited with mounting frustration as the untidy French column, repeatedly halting and re-starting, passed to take the van — as Montauban had insisted. It threatened to be midmorning before the Rifles reached the causeway bridge, and they were impatient with a shuffling, cattlelike progress when they might be jog-trotting ahead in their customary skirmishing role. In Calcutta the fifty-two volunteers from the 1st Battalion had been issued with the improved short Enfield of the 2nd and abandoned their campaign-stained drills for the new regimentals of the 1859 regulation — a black, felt shako with bronzed metal fittings, tunic of dark green with red and black facings, greatcoat of grey. The old epaulettes and wings had disappeared, a welcome improvement, but the uniform's green dye, as before, was already fading under exposure to sun and rain. Within a few more weeks the battalion's appearance would present every shade from straw to jaundiced snuff.

'Why anyone wants ter fight over a soddin' place like *this*,' Dando eyed the surrounding mudflats morosely, 'don't make bleedin' sense.' It was an observation that common soldiers had made, and would continue to make, for hundreds of years. 'When we've got it, what do we *do* wiv it?'

Holloran was less critical of the machinations of Authority than was Dando. Holloran seldom calculated beyond the immediate. Philosophically, the inevitable would not be changed by questioning it and, given his rations, billet, a weekly opportunity to get roaring drunk and enjoy an occasional, convulsive hour with a sweating woman, Holloran was reasonably content. To question ye' betters, bedad, ye had to be educated.

Dando, now, was educated. For three years he had been taught Reading, Writing, a smattering of Arithmetic, and Scripture, by the Society for the Relief of Destitute Young Persons. It was true that, since fending for himself from the age of nine, the advantages of education had achieved him little except that, on behalf of his less fortunate fellows, he could read bottle labels, brothel signs, and count his change. That being so, Holloran conceded without rancour, made Dando a superior person.

'It's maps what does it,' Dando pronounced. 'There's bleedin' big spaces on maps that ain't filled in, see? An' anyone 'oo gits another soddin' space wi' "British Territ'ry" written on it gits made a belted earl an' a Member o' Parliament.' The vast sub-continent of India had recently been transferred to Crown control after the East India Company had been rescued from bloody dispossession by a few thousand men like Dando and Holloran. But men did not enlist to serve a Queen who displayed little interest in their welfare and, indeed, was said to resist any reform that promised to improve their lot, nor to extend still further the boundaries of an empire that was already the biggest the world had seen. They enlisted to escape unemployment, hunger and cold, debt or a demanding woman, and seldom stopped cursing the day that they had. 'The trouble wi' maps,' went on Dando, 'is that in London they don't show the mud an' the festerin' stink.' Nor, he might have added, the thirst and the cracked lips, the flies, blood, dysentery, cholera, or the countless, shallow graves scattered from frozen Canada to the pollution of Kowloon.

From the far right — the direction of the now disappeared 2nd Division — came the sudden rumble of artillery fire. The officers' glasses were out immediately. 'Twelve-pounders — who'll lay a sovereign?' offered Lieutenant Heathcote, but nobody disputed a man who had won a Victoria Cross at the gate of Delhi. North-westward, beyond a line of joss-poles and still more grave-mounds, black smoke was rising. Moments later, from the same direction, came the faint but unmistakable chutter of rifle fire.

Ahead, a French two-pounder mountain battery was wheeling off the causeway, leftward, followed by a Madrassi rocket battery, their wheels biting into firm clay. Company by company, the French infantrymen were also deploying to flank, with the shouted orders being passed along the subsequent column of tramping British. 'Left shoulders forward. Companies in succession to form extended order on the right flank. Milward's half-battery to the front, supported by two companies of the Buffs.'

Major Rigaud, senior officer of the leading four companies of the 60th, took time to light a cheroot as he watched the red-coated Royals clambering from the raised causeway, unslinging their guns. The bandsmen of the 31st, having just struck up the opening bars of 'A Southerly Wind and a Cloudy Sky', were now trotting away towards the field hospital cart to exchange their drums and trumpets for canvas stretchers. 'Three, Four, Five and Six Companies' — Rigaud shouted — 'load ball. Fix swords. Don't fire, men, until you see the whites of their eyes.'

'The whites o' their bleedin' wot?' Dando snorted. ''Ow near does a slant-eyed soddin' Chinaman git before yer sees the whites of 'is bleedin' eyes?'

*

To the rear, the commissariat wagons had lurched to a halt, unable to move forward or backward with their loads of horse-fodder, salt beef, ship's biscuits, condensed milk, pickles and rum. Surgeon-Major Telfer, dismounted, grinned at his subordinate, Surgeon Rennie. 'Do you read history, Rennie?'

Rennie was surprised. 'A little, sir. Occasionally.'

Telfer nodded. 'It's damn' odd, y'know, how we stick to the useless precedents of the past — and especially in war. Look at our cavalrymen, for instance — every one with a damn' great sabre banging around his knees and getting in his way. Why do we always assume that a cavalryman must have a sword?' He paused. 'Do you suppose the Horse Guards have ever considered that a surgeon who treats battle wounds might be a better judge of weapon efficiency than the Select Committee on Ordnance?'

Rennie shrugged, chuckling. 'I'll take the point, sir, but I doubt whether the Commander-in-Chief would take kindly to having the Ordnance Department dictated to by a few bone-setters in uniform who aren't even members of their regiments' messes. Armies are run by precedent, regulations, and the lash — not logic.'

'Ah, but as a surgeon, Rennie, I have a certain clinical interest in what weapons can and cannot do, dammit. When I was a raw young Assistant-Surgeon I thought I'd see men butchered to pieces with these cavalry swords. Well' — he grinned again — 'I'll make a confession. After the Kaffir business, then the Alma, Inkerman, and the Redan, I have *not yet seen* a genuine sabre wound! But cavalrymen still trot around with those damn' medieval frog-stickers and talk gibberish about the science of war! The only thing a sabre is good for is cutting firewood, toasting bread and digging refuse pits.'

Rennie nodded. 'And the new breech-loading guns?'

'That's a lot different. There was a time, young Rennie, when field guns could come up to the front, even in advance of their own infantry, and blaze away without hindrance — until the infantry got the rifle. Then the artillery had to move back, out of range. Now, with the rifled field-gun, they can remain farther back still.' He paused. 'When your grandsons join the Army, Rennie, the only damn' place they'll see a sabre or a bayonet is in the regimental museum. And the enemy they're fighting will be ten miles away. They won't see them either.'

It was all nonsense, Surgeon Rennie mused, but he wasn't going to dispute with an eccentric superior. Guns or no guns, a battle always ended with the infantry bayonet. There was no other possible conclusion to a battle, and there never could be. Whoever heard of fighting an enemy that couldn't be seen?

*

Sir Robert Napier's 2nd Division, on the far right flank, could see its enemy. Two thousand yards ahead were drawn up long, irregular lines of Tartar cavalry, their massed, upright lances, decorated with red-coloured horse-tails, seeming like a forest of grass, scattered with tall banners and long-barrelled gingalls with crews waiting with smoking matches. The noon sun was hot, and the plain shimmered before the eyes, so that the distant horde seemed unreal, a mirage. The Sikh vedettes in the van could hear faint shouts. '*Fan-kwei! Ta! Ta!*'

Napier's infantry had laboriously crossed the mudflats in contiguous columns, halting and re-halting to allow the Coolie Corps with the reserve ammunition wagons to keep pace. It had been a hard slog, and there was an uncomfortable gap of three miles separating them from the causeway and the 1st Division, which by now must be approaching the earthworks of Sinho. Except for vedettes, all of Napier's cavalry — the King's Dragoon Guards in their scarlet tunics and solar helmets, and the turbanned Sikhs — were in echelon on the right, the horses mired to their flanks and blowing.

Milward's half battery of three Armstrong breech-loaders had already been ordered forward, the wheels of guns and caissons clogged and slithering, to open fire at 1,500 yards. It was not to be imagined that the Chinese cranky gingalls would nearly compete at that range, and a throng of correspondents and unattached officers gathered to see the effects of the new guns on a flesh and blood target.

Also new were the shells that Milward's artillerymen were loading. They were cylindrical projectiles embodying a bursting charge and a fulminate detonator, developed by Colonel Jacob of the Scinde Irregular Horse, and a fiendish improvement over the standard muzzle-loaded canister shot. The waiting ranks of San-Ko-Lin-Sin's Tartar cavalry, their own guns hopelessly outranged, were about to be unsuspecting collaborators in the proving of a major advance in military weaponry.

'Ready! FIRE!'

The three guns flashed, roared, and reared backward on their trails, and all eyes followed the flight of the projectiles, clearly discernible. A dozen curious coolies ran, shouting. 'Too many piecee bang, too muchee hot!' Seconds later the hurtling shells burst squarely and accurately among the closely formed Chinese.

At a distance of almost a mile, through the gunsmoke and the distorting influence of the sun's heat, it was difficult to judge the salvo's effect very precisely, even with glasses. There were horses down, and the poles of symbol-scrawled banners swayed and fell, tangling. A dozen gingalls spat from their tripods, impotently, and already Milward's men had flung themselves on their guns, spinning open the screwed breech-blocks.

'Sponge! Reload! Cock ye' locks! Ready?'

The guns lurched again, almost hidden by the powder smoke that remained undispersed in the still, hot air. Behind them, the London correspondents were frantically scribbling the opening lines of their reports of the decimation of the enemy cavalry by the new Armstrongs, and the Cantonese labourers, at a safe distance, were chattering excitedly. The lines of infantry stood sweating, at ease, slapping at flies on reddened necks, taking surreptitious mouthfuls of warm water from their canteens, and wondering if they might be ordered the privilege of lighting their pipes. If the bleedin' gunners were going to fart about all day with a few rag-bag heathens on ponies, then they — the infantry — might as well enjoy a bleedin' pipe o' baccy.

'The beggars are reforming, dammit,' someone said, surprised. The gap torn in the Tartar line had closed, and the banners had risen again. A third salvo burst over the horsemen's heads, and then a fourth, the murderous shell splinters scything down men and kicking animals, vomiting clods of earth skyward. Terrified ponies tugged and reared, and the wretched gingalls were still firing defiantly, the roundshot falling far short of the most advanced British vedettes.

'The yellow devils have got guts, Rennie,' Surgeon-Major Telfer observed. He offered the other his glass. 'But if their general has an ounce of sense he'll not keep them standing there to be chopped down at leisure, b'God. He'll have to pull them back, or attack. We can play this bloody game all day.'

Almost as he spoke there was a commotion in the distant wall of horsemen, and the wings of the massive formation began to peel away to left and right, banners tossing and shouting voices mingling with a confusion of clashing cymbals and drums. Thousands of lance-tips caught the sun, horsehair plumes jostled, and mounted officers urged on their trotting squadrons with gesticulating arms. Slowly at first, but gathering momentum, the two hordes of horsemen, savagely beautiful, began to avalanche towards the flanks of the British position.

'It's an encircling movement,' Telfer said. 'They've got guts, dammit, but not much else. Primitive military leaders are always convinced that if they surround an enemy, they're sure to win. It worked for Hannibal, but he never met a disciplined infantry square, Rennie —'

On the right, Sterling's battery of muzzle-loading nine-pounders exploded into action, their crews jealous of the interest shown the new Armstrongs, and simultaneously the Madrassi rocket battery of the left opened fire with a deafening roar. Momentarily the leading ranks of the advancing Tartars were lost in smoke, but they emerged through it, trotting determinedly, and already the infantrymen of the advanced picquets were scuttling back to the safety of the main position, where the 67th Foot, supplemented by a company of Marines, were forming square, loading, ramming, and standing ready to receive. Behind the impassive, tobacco-chewing redcoats huddled a score of Cantonese coolies, torn between their terror of the approaching Tartar thousands and their reluctance to abandon the safety of the British lines.

Telfer and Rennie, standing at their horses' heads on a small mound, were suddenly and uncomfortably aware that they were alone, that nobody stood between them and the thundering mass of Tartar cavalry. The corpulent Telfer, shouting for Rennie to follow, abandoned dignity and ran for the nearest British troops, but Rennie, unwilling to lose his horse, attempted to tug the animal in his wake. The hard-mouthed Talien-wan gelding complied reluctantly, confused by the noise and the wild shots of the galloping Tartars that tore up the clay about its feet. Only yards from the sanctuary of the Marines' ranks, the British square opened fire, and the maddened beast reared, eyes rolling, flinging the obdurate Rennie in all directions. 'For God's sake, man — let the damn' thing go!' Telfer roared. Several Marines, more apprehensive of the horse's lashing hooves than the approaching enemy, jabbed with their bayonets, and in a moment the crazed beast was churning and careering away to the accompaniment of the redcoats' ironic cheers. Surgeon Rennie, on hands and knees, thrust himself between the legs of the laughing, sweating soldiers.

At four hundred yards, faced with the remorseless, controlled volleys of rifle-fire, the Tartars lost cohesion and, with it, their determination. Some halted, milling confusedly, others scattered, alone or in small groups, screeching, with lances waving. Seventy or eighty reached within yards of Sterling's battery, but wheeled away when charged by a troop of Sikhs. On the far right the King's Dragoon Guards drew their sabres and a trumpet teetered, almost lost among the noise of musketry.

'Trot! Trot out! Hold ye' dressing!'

Glorious in scarlet, blue and gold, with only their bearskins substituted by white solar helmets, sabres outstretched with the knuckles of every hand turned upward, the squadrons of Dragoon Guards rolled forward, followed by the blue serge tunics and red cummerbunds of the Sikh Horse. The Tartars, showing superb horsemanship, were turning away, twisting in their saddles to fire their matchlocks, then reloading as they galloped. Their shaggy ponies outstripped the heavy cavalry chargers with impertinent ease, carrying their riders, within minutes, beyond the hovels of Sinho and the distant trench-lines, and leaving their ill conditioned pursuers blown and exhausted.

The Divisional Commander, Sir Robert Napier, mopped his neck with a bandana. 'We haven't exactly covered ourselves with glory, have we?' he sniffed. 'With the taxpayers providing us with rifled breech-loading guns — all six of 'em — someone in Westminster's going to ask why a few thousand mounted savages couldn't be massacred to a man. If I'm any judge' — he shaded his eyes — 'there's not above three hundred dead, after all that noise.' After two Sikh wars and the Mutiny, he was an expert judge. He shrugged, then nodded at an aide. 'All right — sound off "General Advance". It looks as though Sinho is open.'

*

But not quite. On the left, nearer to Sinho, the 1st Division had deployed into position before advancing on the entrenchments and mud walls of the village. At a thousand yards both British and French guns opened fire, untroubled by the flaring gingalls and scattered matchlock shots of the enemy. There seemed to be a considerable number of cavalry in and around the defences, but with no apparent sense of order, riding about and firing their guns aimlessly. 'They'd do a lot bleedin' better,' Dando observed, 'if they stopped fartin' about like pimps in a fairground.'

'Shure,' Holloran agreed, 'an' ef they kep' still.'

Somewhere ahead, an artillery bugler was blowing 'Extend', and the guns were relimbering. A French officer drew his sword and was pointing it, dramatically, at Sinho. '*Bataillon! Par sections, en ligne! Marche!*'

'An' before yer tell us, Dando,' Sergeant Garvin said, 'that's French for "Stow yer gab, git orf yer arse, an' march yerself back ter the bridge an' see wot's 'appened ter the soddin' ration cart".'

Dando spat. 'If there's one thing I 'ate more than Bengali gun-bullocks —'

But Major Rigaud had tossed away his cheroot. 'Three, Four, Five and Six Companies! In line of companies, at the short trail — Forwaard!'

'And that includes the damn' Indian yallers,' snorted Lieutenant Shaw.

*

Lieutenant Shaw's earliest acquaintanceship with the 'yallers' had been in Calcutta. He had seen at a distance the fifty-two volunteers from the home-going 1st Battalion wheel on to the drill-ground of Fort William — lean men, bearded, as brown as natives, in ragged hot-weather drills and battered kepis, most in broken boots and equipment tied with string. He had heard a great deal of the *Shaitan-ke-Pultan*, of how they had routed five thousand sepoys under Mirza Abu Bakr at the Hindun crossing, then led the bloody assault on the Kashmir Gate of Delhi, collecting five Victoria Crosses in the process. Their officer, Lieutenant Alfred Heathcote, looked no less a vagrant than any of his men, and his familiar relationship with the ordinary soldiers Shaw found disconcerting. It was not the thing for an officer to sit on the ground among the rankers, sharing their tobacco and their coarse conversation — and, dammit, actually examining their blistered feet with his own hands. Discipline demanded that an officer should remain insular and aloof, communicating his orders, whenever possible, through the medium of a sergeant. Familiarity bred contempt, and worse. It was mildly annoying that Shaw saw not the slightest suggestion of contempt for Heathcote among the yallers.

Shaw also doubted the wisdom of dispersing the Indian yallers throughout the entire battalion. He had always thought that a pestilence should be confined, quarantined, not allowed to undermine the stability of every damn' company, including his own.

And he had been passing one of his own barrack-rooms when he heard the explosion of shouted, obscene abuse from within, which could be only that of a man in the grip of extreme rage and frustration. The sergeant's voice had followed, demanding silence and an explanation, and then Shaw recognised the incensed and plaintive voice of one of his own men.

'It was *'im* — bleedin' Dando! We'd jes' bobbed out our ration, see? Beef an' taters. Then this soddin' yaller sez, "Grace? Don't you bleedin' griffins in the Second Battalion say grace? Don't yer know it's a soddin' regimental custom?" So we sez grace, see?' The voice choked. 'An' when I opens me eyes, me bleedin' beef's gorn!'

7

There was little in Sinho to compensate for the Allies' wearying march from Pehtang. Two narrow, muddy lanes, flanked by a canal, stretched for a half mile before dissolving into the open plain that extended southward to the Pei-ho river. Many of the inhabitants remained, the little, trousered women turning their backs on the soldiers to avoid the evil eye of the foreign devils who, in turn, lost no time in transferring everything edible — poultry, pigs, vegetables — into their camp kettles. The Cantonese coolies, having recovered their courage at the disappearance of the Tartar cavalry, were busily engaged in rifling the clothing of enemy dead. 'Inglish velly blave!' they shouted elatedly at passing British, and miming the firing of a gun, 'Ping pung Tartar wello!'

In fact, the number of enemy dead was disappointingly small in exchange for several hundred rounds of nine-and twelve-pounder ammunition and several thousand rifle bullets. The reason, somebody explained, was that the Chinese did not fight in tight, ordered formations like civilised troops, but as a dispersed rabble, so that an exploding shell killed only two or three instead of a dozen. As evidence they pointed to the corpse of a Chinese gunner who had been cut in half by a direct hit from an Armstrong shell which, however, had left unmarked the gingall he had been serving. Perhaps, the pundits suggested, the Armstrongs were just too damn' accurate?

Whatever the reason, the action before Sinho had been depressingly inconclusive. Nobody appreciated that more than Sir Hope Grant. Given room to manoeuvre, he might have outflanked the Chinese and given them no chance to fall back on their Taku forts. Other generals fought on wide, dry terrain, like the Indian Doab, or the Alma Heights, where brigades could be disposed like chess-pieces as in a Hyde Park Review. He, Grant, had the injustice of fifteen miles of nightmarish Chinese mud which turned his orders into lotteries, the commissariat into a shambles, and allowed a horde of mounted hooligans to thumb their noses at the best troops in the world.

The best troops in the world — or, at least, two of them — also lacked enthusiasm for Sinho. The village had been quickly and systematically stripped of everything remotely of value by the French — foodstuffs, livestock, liquor, bedding and clothing — and the natives that remained, evicted from their houses, roamed the camp-lines, begging food scraps or a few cash. The Cantonese coolies treated their impoverished countrymen with contempt, the French with kicks and rifle-butts, and the English with shrugs of indifference. Only the Irishmen, with their memories of starvation and eviction, displayed occasional sympathy. A score of Tartar wounded were being cared for in the hospital tents.

But the resources of Sinho were totally inadequate for the needs of 15,000 Europeans. Local water was undrinkable, and had to be hauled continually over the narrow causeway from Pehtang, itself in short supply — and water being more important than most other commodities, the men's rations had reverted to the familiar level of pork and biscuit.

And then there was the dust. Beyond the mudflats, the open plain stretched endlessly westward, and from it a fierce, sirocco-like wind carried a fine, powdery dust that filled every crevice, stung eyes and gritted in teeth. Windows, doors or tent-flaps offered no protection. The dust penetrated everywhere, covering food, blankets, papers, and spreading inches deep over the plain, requiring only the slightest provocation to rise, swirling and choking.

'There was dust at Alipore,' reminisced Dando, 'but there was a bleedin' booze-tent in Alipore.'

Holloran nodded. 'An' wimmin.'

'Poxed ter the eyebrows.' Dando dismissed the women. 'There was booze, even if it was soddin' coach-varnish. Yer could git blind, screamin' *gkazi* fer a rupee.'

'Fer wan rupee,' Holloran agreed, 'ye cud get rale *toight*, so ye cud.' He sighed. 'Thim wuz the days.'

'If yer 'ad a '*undred* rupees in Sinho,' Dando went on, 'yer couldn't buy a sniff of a barmaid's bleedin' swab-rag.'

'Faith, ye cudn't,' said Holloran.

For want of something better to do, they had walked beyond the last of the high-pointed houses, roofed with thatch or matting, beyond the sites of the orchards in which every fruit tree had been chopped down for firewood, and the old Tartar camp where now only a few ragged shreds of canvas flapped in the wind. On the left of the track was the canal, as clay-coloured as the Pei-ho from which it flowed, rising and falling with every tide. The wind-blown dust rustled like rain among the reeds.

Suddenly Holloran halted. 'The Divil! Wid thet be a *ship* on the wather, me ol' Dando?'

Dando shaded his eyes from the dust. 'It's a junk — painted wi' bleedin' flowers.'

It was, indeed, a small junk, with lateen sails lowered, tied at the canal's edge to which it was also linked by a plank. Unlike the many native craft they had seen on the Pei-ho river, however, this one was garishly painted with flowers, birds and fish, its stern house hung with paper lanterns and garlands. The boat sat motionless in the dirty water, suggesting that, with the tide low, it was temporarily aground.

But Dando and Holloran were not the first to chance upon the oddly-decorated junk. Three French infantrymen were emerging from the stern house, heavily laden with bundled silks and furs, brass kettles and pots, quilts and embroidered cushions. Behind them several Chinese women followed, wailing.

It was not an unusual proceeding. They had seen the like scores of times in Pehtang and Sinho, and although they might have experienced pity for some shabby peasant robbed of his last pig or fowl, they entertained little for the owner of a large and apparently valuable boat — particularly one painted with flowers. The *Infanterie de la Marine*, however, represented a provocation that neither could resist. When the leading, burdened Frenchman stepped from the plank, he found himself faced by Patrick Holloran.

'Ye're a black-mouthed scutt ev a frog-eatin' bastard,' Holloran said, then thrust his face forward. 'Whit are ye?'

The Frenchman did not understand the words, but he accurately interpreted the tone. He spat. '*Bruyant. Ecartez-vous.*'

Holloran glanced at Dando. 'Whit did he say?'

''Ee sez,' Dando explained, 'yer' a shit-faced gutter-rat of a syphilitic Orangeman, an' yer can kiss 'is bleedin' arse.'

'Orangeman?' Holloran's jaw dropped. '*Orangeman?*' He removed his shako carefully. 'Hould me hat, me ol' Dando.' He spat on his hands. 'Niver let ut be said,' he told the Frenchman, 'thet Patrick Holloran starrted anythin', bedad. I only hets whin I'm het.' He pointed to his jaw.

'Het me.' Dando, having seated himself resignedly on a large rock, began to fill his pipe.

The Frenchman snorted, flung his armful of plunder to the ground, lowered his head and charged. He was a big man, and Holloran, who had lifted his fists in the approved prize-fighter fashion, was completely foiled. He was flung backwards, sprawling in the dust and, before he could struggle to a sitting position, his adversary's heavy boot crunched into his ribs.

Dando shook his head. 'I wouldn't 'ave that.' He struck a match and cupped it over the bowl of his pipe.

The Frenchman laughed. '*Essayez de ne pas oublier la leçon, cochon*! *Ouste!*' He grinned over his shoulder at his fellows. '*Vennez-vous?*'

Holloran climbed to his feet. 'Faith, an' now ye've made me lose me temper, an' thet's a terrible thing, so 'tis. Hev ye ever heard ev Lámfhada ev the Long Arrm?'

The Frenchman had not. He was half-stooped in the process of retrieving his spoil when the bunched, rock-like fist of Holloran split his nose from brow to lip like a burst plum. The man gave a strangled yelp, sank to his knees, then slowly fell on his face, the blood frothing from his mouth. Behind him, his following companions had no opportunity to disencumber themselves before a berserk tornado sent one spinning into the muddy shallows of the canal and the other, stunned and helpless, on all fours, among a jumble of cushions and kettles. Holloran licked his skinned knuckles.

'It took yer bleedin' long enough,' Dando said.

'Shure, an' I'm gettin' soft,' Holloran agreed ruefully. 'We've not had a good foight since thet bloddy Fusilier spat in ye' beer in Benares.' He sighed. 'Thimi wuz the days.'

The three Frenchmen were struggling to their feet. Dando rose. 'Orl right, mon-bleedin'-sweers. Yer can pissey-orf, *ek dum* — or *I'll* start on yer. An' if *I* start on yer, yer'll be needin' yer frogs minced fer a bleedin' month.'

Holloran raised his fists again, bouncing on his toes. 'Bedad, an' I'll blast ye through the top ev *Tir na nOc*, so I will — one at a toim, or all at once —'

The objects of his threat, however, did not share his belligerence. They turned away towards Sinho, pausing at a safe distance to hurl back incomprehensible insults, whereupon Holloran again bounced on his toes, his fists striking at the air and returning equally incomprehensible references to Lug, Dug, and Bendegeit Bran. 'When yer've finished,' Dando said wearily, ''ere's yer 'at. And yer've got a 'ole in the arse of yer breeches.'

A small, elderly Chinese woman, trousered and pigtailed, bowed before them. '*Hsieh, hsieh.*' Five or six other women stood on the deck of the junk, nodding and smiling.

'If yer arst me,' Dando decided, 'it's a bleedin' floatin' whore-shop.'

'Glory be,' Holloran straightened his shako. 'Es me ol' friend, Mulvaney ev the 83rd, used ter say, "Het an man an' help a woman, an' ye can't be far wrong, bedad."'

The woman was still bowing, throwing an inviting hand towards the gang-plank of the junk. '*T'ai-t'ai hsiang ch'ih shih-mo fan?*'

Dando, for once, was right. The oddly-painted craft was a flower-boat, a floating brothel from up-river Tien-tsin, and to any brothel an army in the field meant women-starved men with pockets jingling — foreign devils or not. Dando and Holloran stepped gingerly over the plank to the deck, the younger women, on their tiny feet, bowing, retreating, gigging. The older woman hovered in their wake, ushering them aft towards the stern house. '*Hao! Hao!*'

'She's the Mother Judger,' Dando said. 'She sez she wants ter measure yer fer size, Irish. She's goin' ter think yer' a bleedin' freak — Holloran o' the Third Leg.'

The stern house was lit by a dozen small oil lamps behind coloured glasses, their reek mingling with that of generously sprinkled perfume that snatched at the throat. Deep cushions littered the deck-space, surrounding a polished, inches-high table, and tapestries masked the bulkheads, effectively forbidding all entrance of outside air. It was stiflingly warm and, presented with cups of hot wine, poured from a kettle, the two men's sweat burst from their pores, soaking their shirts.

They sat cross-legged, their cups repeatedly filled, eyeing the dishes of food appearing before them — sponge cakes, unidentifiable meats, shellfish, soup, bamboo heads, chopped vegetables. Holloran took up a dark green, faecaloid-shaped sea-slug between finger and thumb. 'Bedad, it looks loik a bloddy turrd.' He sampled it cautiously. 'The Divil! Et is a bloddy turrd!'

'I s'pose,' Dando nodded, 'yer've got a palate fer turds.'

A space had been cleared among the foodstuffs on the table, and on to it climbed one of the women. She bowed to them both, eyes downcast, then pushed her trousers from her hips, over her knees to her ankles, and stepped free of them. For several seconds she agitated her navel suggestively, sat on her heels with knees wide-splayed, and finally turned on all fours, her brow to the table and her buttocks raised and churning.

'B'Jasus,' breathed Holloran, 'hev ye iver seen anythin' loik ut?'

'Plenty ov times,' Dando sniffed, 'but not wiv the bleedin' cow-'eel an' pickles.' The sweet, cloying wine was more potent than they had thought, and they watched with growing torpidity as the gyrating woman on the table was replaced by a second and then a third. The old woman stood, still nodding and smiling. '*Ting la? Pu?*'

'It makes a change, though,' Dando conceded, 'from the bleedin' barricks canteen. If we 'ad proper booze instead o' this prune-juice and liquorice, and a basin o' stew'd eels instead o' this seaweed —'

'Dando, me jewel,' agreed Holloran, 'shure, ye cud charrm the magic from a thrush's throat —'

Dando suddenly sat upright. ''Ere — Irish!' He pointed. 'Wot was yer blarneyin' about Chinese wimmin? Yer said they was soddin' different —'

Holloran shook off a haze of inebriation, peering. 'Bedad, an' ye're roight. Thet's the same es two pays, so ut is!'

'We've been bleedin' cheated,' said Dando.

Holloran nodded. 'Et's a bloddy dishgrace — chatin' honust sodgers. Faith, an' we shud axe fer our money back. It's enough ter turrn an Aythiopian whoit.'

'Yer'd think, comm' orl the way ter soddin' China,' Dando resumed, 'they'd 'ave the decency —'

'The *dacincy* —'

'— ter prervide proper booze, an' wimmin wiv reg'lashun feet, an' proper Chinese glut-pieces —'

'Rig'lation fate,' Holloran affirmed. 'Bedad, there's been bloddy wars fought fer less —'

'There was the War o' Jenkins' ear-'ole, fer a bleedin' start,' Dando considered.

'Shure — an' whin the baggage camel stud on O'Leary's thumb —'

‘There was that brothel in the Sudder Bazaar, in Meerut, see —’ Dando pronounced, then halted. A woman knelt at his side and was fumbling with the front fastening of his breeches. ‘Soddin’ ’ell — ain’t nuthin’ sacred?’

Holloran, similarly assailed, was philosophical. ‘Faith, an’ there’s no resishtance left in me. Ef ye’re determined on carnality, shure, oi’ll help ye wid me buttons, me darlint —’

*

Rifleman Joseph Dando had known his women. Every Queen’s soldier knew the wheedling prostitutes who ‘followed the drum’, from Plymouth to Inverness, thronging the barracks’ gate or haunting the garrison-town taverns, gin-soaked and starved, and desperate for a shilling patron before the drums beat retreat. And after a few years in India, every Queen’s soldier knew that Rohikund women were hot and easy, that Madras women grunted and scratched, Bengalis were barrels of nails, Punjabis churned like gun-mules, and show a Patna woman a rupee and she’d be on her back quicker than a whip. Dando had known them all, but he’d forgotten most.

Two of them he would always remember — Hannah Minting of Croydon, and Padmini of the Sudder Bazaar.

Hannah Minting, the diminutive, brazen young female, whose likeness could be met by the score in Aldershot, Dublin, Woolwich or Portsmouth, had been Joseph’s first. He was sixteen, and he had never seen a woman unclothed before — unless you counted those pallid, marble statues at which men looked as if they were only lamp-posts, and at which ladies seldom looked at all.

On the bed he reached for her clumsily, at her breasts and then the warm velvet below her belly. She eased him away amusedly, looking at him with half-closed eyes. ‘Take it quiet, Joey, or yer’ll go orf bang before yer’ve even started.’ He did go off bang, as soon as her cool, experienced fingers led him to her. He jerked, his throat swelling, ashamed, but she lay still until his agitation had passed. ‘Now, we’ll take it quiet, Joey — like I said. Yer’ll never git yer shillin’-worth if yer kettle boils too quick, see?’

Then it had been different. She played him expertly, with caressing fingertips and the pressure of her thighs, one moment soothing his excitement, and then subtly provoking again until, at last, he would be denied no longer, but came to her with all the pent-up voracity of a young animal. And now she submitted to his frenzy, and when he was finally sated she held his hot face against her breast until his racing heart quietened. He had never realised that it was going to be like this — one moment brutal with lust and, the next, a drained husk. Was it always finished as quickly?

The novelty of an unclothed Hannah, not enhanced by her devotion to the gin bottle, quickly palled. It was difficult to revere a woman who tolerated his presence in her crumpled bed only when there were no paying customers, and evicted him with obscenities when there were. Her morning appearances, puffed of face, tangle-haired, bad-tempered and reeking of stale alcohol, could not long sustain his youthful infatuation. Even so, Hannah Minting, the flint-hard little prostitute, had been his first, and had taught him much. 'Wimmin ain't bleedin' plough-'orses,' she lectured him. 'It's orlright wi' wimmin like me. 'Arf the time we 'ave ter wrestle wi' drink-sodden bears, but if yer ever 'ave a woman of yer own, Joey —'

A woman of his own? It was a possibility he had never remotely considered, before or since.

But since, there had been Padmini. He had found her in the hot, ramshackle Sudder Bazaar in Meerut, in the *Kama-ledhiplava* — the Boat in an Ocean of Love. Padmini had been different to the others, with their betel-stained teeth and jewelled noses, their hawking and spitting, and their repertoire of barrack-room language, Padmini had been different.

A thousand years before, the artisan whose hands had chiselled the lovely Ushas, Daughter of Heaven, must have known well the warm, exquisite body of a Padmini — small, sinuous, orb-breasted, shaven of hair and saffron dusted. The nails of her toes and fingers were tinted with alacktaka, a slim bangle on each ankle and wrist, and when she loosened the girdle at her waist, her saree floated to her feet like a gauzy mist. Padmini lifted her satiny arms proudly. 'How will you have me, Dando-sahib? The ram, the turn-about, the he-goat, the rainbow arch? There are twenty-five ways. The wife of Indra? The yawn?'

Padmini was the eternal woman of India — submissive but not servile, learned in the sixty-four accomplishments of Kama Shastra, of the arts of embracing, of kissing, pressing and biting, of the twenty-five variations of congress, and the appropriate sighs and sounds of tenderness and passion. She had that quality of the practised concubine of persuading her man of the hour that he was the only one that had ever mattered, melancholy at his departure, and awaiting his return with yearning. And she had cost three rupees, an expensive luxury for an ordinary soldier.

'What have you known but your damp fish of white women, Dando-sahib, with their hairy armpits and hairy *yoni*, and pale, sweating skin that the sun has never kissed? Do they not lie on their backs like sacks of flour, staring at the ceiling and waiting for the offence to be finished?' She placed the palms of her hands together. 'The lotus position, Dando-sahib? The jump of a hare?'

*

'Wot was your'n like, Irish?' enquired Dando. They negotiated the plank carefully.

'Loik a bloddy stame-engine,' Holloran said, 'wid me underneath. I'll be needin' a wake ter recover me strength, so I will.'

'A week o' bleedin' pack-drill,' said Sergeant Garvin. With two men of the duty picquet, he eyed them from the canal bank. 'Fer assaultin' three of our gallant allies o' the *Infanterie de la Marine*, not ter mention partakin' of a drunken orgy, *and* torn breeches.' He shook his head sadly. 'Lieutenant Shaw's duty officer, an' he's walkin' up an' down, readin' QRs, like a starved tiger — but laughin' to 'imself.'

8

The news of the foreign devils' landing, and of the great battle of Sinho in which they had been slaughtered in their thousands by the invincible Tartar cavalry, had passed through Tien-tsin on its way to Peking. There were, it was said, a pitiful few foreign survivors of the action, but these would quickly be put to the sword, or ordered to surrender, and then Tien-tsin would see the barbarians in cages dragged through the city, broken and humiliated. There would be fire-crackers and prancing dragons, and the mandarins in their litters would throw sweetmeats to the gutter-urchins who thrust at the prisoners with sharpened sticks.

True, the news did not explain the dozens of ragged deserters from the *luh-ying* who had reached the outskirts of Tien-tsin, hunted down by cavalry and beheaded immediately. If several dozen had managed to reach Tien-tsin before being overtaken, how many had fled from Sinho?

And Fung Yu-lan, the notary to the Council, who had spent seven years in Hong Kong and spoke the barbarians' language, had sucked his teeth doubtfully. He had seen the foreigners' great iron ships in the anchorage off Victoria, the polished guns on wheels, and the columns of soldiers marching in step, all with precisely similar red faces and whiskers, and all given numbers so that they could be distinguished apart even by their own officers. He had seen them roaring, fighting drunk among the hovels of Happy Valley, but he had also seen them disciplined, machine-like in their obedience. It was not true that only the Tartars stank worse than the British, and Fung Yu-lan was aware of the notorious fairy-tale quality of despatches written by Chinese generals who, for reasons of 'face', turned skirmishes into epic battles, defeats into victories, and blithely ignored every impending hazard until it became an inescapable disaster. Fortunately, Chinese generals had previously only been matched against other Chinese generals, so that ineptitude had been cancelled out by ineptitude. Now, if Peking persisted in believing that if the British were ignored they somehow did not exist, then a great deal more would be lost than just face.

P'u Sung Ling, Mandarin of the Plain Glass Button, was reluctant to listen to the sacrilegious utterings of Fung Yu-lan — whose services he utilised often, since writing with six-inch fingernails encased in silver sheaths was not only degrading but almost impossible. It was also impossible that the Son of Heaven, in Peking, could be wrong.

Fung Yu-lan had been a shoopan — a mere clerk — in British pay. What was his knowledge of military matters beside that of the exalted San-Ko-Lin-Sin? The forts of Taku were impregnable; they had never been taken, and during recent months they had been heavily strengthened. Even — the mandarin winced mentally — even in the inconceivable event of the Taku forts falling to the barbarians, there was still Tien-tsin between them and Peking. Tien-tsin had walls sixty feet high, wide enough for three wagons to drive abreast, surmounted by battlements and loopholes and, at frequent intervals, crenelated towers of twice the wall height. P'u Sung Ling had a sudden, uneasy thought. Whether the barbarians came as captives in bamboo cages, or as conquering invaders, they were coming to Tien-tsin. If the former, then there was no problem. If the latter, then, for certain, the British general could be bought off. All generals could be bought. What would a British general demand? Five thousand taels of silver? Ten thousand?

And if the British general was either too demanding, or incorruptible — and the latter possibility was almost unbelievable — his second-in-command would undoubtedly have ambitions to be first. All subordinates did, and it might be arranged. What kind of men were these, to be ruled by a portly little middle-aged woman? In China, women were kept in their rightful place, and did not even lift their eyes to a man's. The idea of a woman ruling men, and being superior even to her own husband, was preposterous, unnatural, and a wickedness.

*

Yü had never heard of Queen Victoria. She had never seen any foreign barbarians and had heard only fleeting references to them. They had an evil eye and were bad joss, hairy faces, and they were uncivilised. That was all she had heard. Female menials did not share conversations, even with other menials.

In any case, her days were too full for thought to be given to nebulous foreigners. There were floors to be sponged, vegetables cleaned — onions, lettuce, radishes — and sucking pigs dragged from their sows' bellies for the kitchen, and she would be sore and bleeding from Tien Mu's bamboo switch if she lazed in her chores. There was infants' urine to be collected for the Master's mouth-wash, taken to him by others in a delicate porcelain cup, with fragrant green tea — Twankay, Hyson, Imperial — followed by his breakfast of tiny pastries — *dim sum* — filled with fish or pork, shrimp and chicken, deep-fried or steamed. She saw the Master only rarely, and when she did she must drop to her knees and press her forehead to the ground. In his richly brocaded gown, his satin boots with white soles, with his jewelled fingers, he was a vision of magnificence to awe a female menial. It was impossible that his eyes even noticed her, and she trembled with fear that they might. It was said that he still took young concubines to warm his thin frame and to deferentially submit to his jade stem if he so condescended. That, when Yü dared consider it, must surely represent the ultimate in happiness, and she shivered, and breathed quickly. But a female menial with unbound feet could not dream of the jade stem of a mandarin. More likely one of the litter-coolies, or the pig-keeper, would decide that, despite her feet, it was time for her flowery path to be broached. Would she resist, on that first occasion? She did not know. She had heard the other women whispering, giggling, of the attributes of this man or that, of meetings in the shaded flood-ditch, and she had watched the frenzy of the old, tusked boar when put to a sow, and the men laughing.

Occasionally, alone, when collecting urine from one of the household's several infants, she opened her clothes and placed the child's mouth to the nipple of a young breast, seething with a strange, indefinable yearning as the lusty sucking brought a lump to her throat and a contortion to her belly. But it was not, she knew secretly, the frustrated mouth of an infant that she wanted, but a jade stem. If she did not have one soon, she would begin to grow sour and ill-tempered, like Tien Mu.

It was perhaps almost inevitable that the first man to take notice of a woman with unbound feet would be one with a warped taste. Kiaking, the strange one, had been in subdued mood for many weeks, and the wariness towards him that Yü shared with the other women had relaxed. She was flinging scraps to the fowls when she saw him approaching, and this time she did not, as she would once, hasten to seek the safety of another's company.

From a distance of several yards, Kiaking surveyed her in silence, then glanced about him. There was nobody in sight. He moved into the hedged alleyway that led to the house, effectively blocking her retreat. 'Come here,' he said. There was a bubble of saliva in the corner of his mouth.

Yü placed down her pannier and went to him, her eyes on the ground and her heart pounding, but whether from terror or ecstasy she was too distracted to decide. She stood, not daring to lift her gaze to his.

For a long minute of agony he made no movement. She could hear him sucking breath between his teeth, and then he reached forward to grasp her pigtail, twisting her face upwards, roughly. His eyes were reddening.

'Have you tasted man-fruit, girl?'

Dumbly, she shook her head. This, then, was the moment. What matter if he was Kiaking, the strange one? Was he not the son of the Master? What other women, so unworthy and with ugly feet, could hope for such privilege? Others said that Kiaking was an animal in his lusting, that he enjoyed inflicting pain, but what was a little pain in exchange for such happiness?

He released her pigtail. 'Kowtow,' he ordered. She dropped to her knees, her forehead lowered. Would it be here, between the bushes? Should she remove her faded, nankeen trousers — now?

'Now,' he said.

Yü looked up. Kiaking held his jade stem between his hands, and it was an object of supreme beauty and elegance, of majesty. This, then, was why men were superior to women. Now she knew. Her mouth was dry, and she felt the wetness of sweat between her thighs.

Yü shuffled forward on her knees towards the son of the Master. What did he desire of her? There were many ways, she had heard, for her flowery path to be entered. She had never been entered by a man, but she knew the positions —

Manner one. Lie upon your back with your thighs raised. Allow your Master between your thighs, to introduce his member into you, pressing your toes into the ground, rummaging, scratching his buttocks

Manner two. Kneel on your knees and elbows, as if in prayer. In this way your flowery path is projected backwards, and he will attack you from the rear

Manner three. Your Master will sit on his heels, with his knees open. You will sit over his thighs, your legs embracing him

Manner four. Embrace with your legs the waist of your Master, who is standing, with your arms passed around his neck. Whilst suspended, your Master will insinuate his member into your flowery path

The wonderful object held her gaze, irresistibly. She choked, fumbling at the cord of her trousers. 'How will my Lord take this unworthy slave?'

His lips were beginning to twist uncontrollably. 'Taste of the man-fruit. Now,'

Yü was puzzled. What did he mean? The wonderful jade stem before her, intoxicating in its arrogance, and there was a yawning want in the pit of her belly —

Kiaking grunted impatiently, grasped her by her ears, and wrenched her head forward. A gouging thumb forced her jaws apart, tearing her lip. He held her, vice-like, against him, and then she was choking, stifled, as he churned savagely, squealing. Yü's nails raked desperately, but he laughed and clenched her tighter, and she sobbed, knowing she could only yield, that there was vomit climbing into her throat, and her senses were failing. Behind her, the fowls scattered.

But Kiaking's squealing was suddenly a surprised screech. Yü found herself flung backwards, sprawling at the feet of Tien Mu — and Mother Lightning's bamboo switch was lashing viciously. Kiaking crouched, reeling, his hands clasped to a wealed face, and cursing.

'Hi yah!' Tien Mu spat. 'Coolie filth! Pig dung!' The switch rose and fell again. 'Is there no end to your lechery? Is not even an underling with ugly feet, and stinking of the kitchen, safe from this abomination?' Yü gulped air into her lungs, her lips broken, nose bleeding.

Kiaking's hands flailed, beating aside the blows. 'Bitch! You old bitch!' He was almost incoherent. 'Am I not the first son of the Master? What matters a miserable coolie-woman? She is of less account than the sweepings from the swine-pen, you stupid hag! Who are you, toothless woman, that you dare confront the son of the Master?'

But old Tien Mu stood firm, her wrinkled face twisting with disgust. 'In the house of your honourable father, the meanest slave is protected. Is he not a mandarin of the Council of Tien-tsin, of utmost dignity and respect, a Reader of the Law, and entrusted with the chop of the divine Lord of Ten Thousand Years? Will you stand before your honourable father and explain your animal filth, and why you insult his First Wife?' Mother Lightning gazed contemptuously at a flaccid jade stem, then spat on it.

Kiaking trembled with rage, swaying, his fingers opening and closing and his eyes beginning to roll. It seemed certain that he would explode, that he would smash the old woman aside, but incredibly he did not. He turned and, hunch-shouldered, walked away, with one leg jerking as it dragged.

Tien Mu drew a deep breath, eyeing Yü. 'You are a little fool, and you deserve whipping as much as he. He can give you nothing but an ocean of tears.' She paused. 'For three weeks you will not feed or sleep with the other people. You will be unclean, and you will be locked in the summerhouse. Three times every day you will rinse your mouth with a broth of boiled ginseng root, and if in three weeks there is no *fan-kwei* sickness, then you will be released. If you have taken the sickness, you will be whipped, your ears cut off, and then thrown into the Pei-ho.'

9

The dun, stratified mass of the fort of Tang Ku was typical of the Taku group beyond it — a three-mile, crenelated wall, terminating at each end on the river bank, and enclosing fortified tower-mounds, lines of huts with arched roofs, a vast cavalry enclosure and, innermost, the huddled houses of a small township, smoke-wreathed and puddled. The wall was additionally surrounded by a shallow wet-ditch and an expanse of embedded, sharpened bamboo stakes, thicker than a man's arm and closely spaced.

The fort's defenders had been variously numbered at between 2,000 and 6,000, its guns forty-five, of calibre up to 24-pounders. Certainly the walls were crowded, planted with long-tailed banners, and officers' glasses had distinguished the white, circular badge of the army of the General of Chihlee. Artillery officers, with their new binoculars, were noting with amused satisfaction the dozens of open, unprotected baskets of powder behind the defending guns.

For most of the preceding night, 500 men of the 60th Rifles had waited in the orchards only 700 yards from the wall, covering the coolies digging shelter trenches for the morning's assault. The Chinese, aware of their presence, had flung fireballs for several hours, picturesque but ineffective.

'Shure, there's people thet pays ter see fireworks,' said Holloran, 'whin orl they hev ter do is join the bloddy Army.'

'An' git paid 7/6d a week,' nodded Dando, 'wiv 5/4d deducted fer food, maint'nance an' necessaries.' He sniffed. 'Jes' wait till my time's expired, that's orl. Pineapples an' a donkey an' cart. Then I'm goin' ter *expand.* Song sheets an' litrercher. It's no soddin' good puttin' capital inter flowers, wot don't larst — 'specially when yer keep 'em under the bed.'

'*Pigs,*' interrupted Holloran. 'Wid a few pigs as well, bedad.' He could not visualise a lucrative future for pineapples and literature in Letterkenny. 'Pigs es the thing, an' ye kin still kape thim under the bed, wid a few praties.'

'*Pigs*? 'Oo the bleedin' 'ell wants *pigs*? Wot d'yer do wiv pigs under the bed?'

'Bedad, ye don't do nuthin'. Thet's the fashinatin' beauty ev it, me ol' Dando. Ye leave thim be, ter make theer own arrangements. An' whin ye heers the ol' sow swearin' loik a haythen, ye goes back ter slape, an' in the mornin', shure, theer's six or siven little pink divils thet'll fetch thirty shillin' apiece in four months.'

It was, indeed, a fascinating prospect, but nor could Dando visualise maintaining six or seven pigs under his bed, in a single room in Kennington, with its peeling, leprous walls, splintered floor, and a single waterpump shared by forty other families. There was bleedin' limits.

He had always tolerated animals, but had never loved them. He remembered the donkey, purchased at Smithfield market for three pounds — his father's most valuable acquisition — and the long tramp to Blackfriars Bridge, thence Covent Garden or Billingsgate, for plaice, bloaters, sprats, oranges and nuts. Winkles sold at penny a pint, oysters at four a penny. Later, when he had been a doctor's lad in rural Merton, there had been Charlie Judd's two giant, gentle plough-horses, with their velvet noses, huge, feathered feet, and warm, hay-smelling breath. But steam-engines were the thing, Charlie Judd had said. Already there were steam-engines that could haul and plough, drive a pump or a wood-saw, and likely they'd soon be picking apples off trees. Likely there'd even be steam cow-milkers, steam butter-churners, and steam bulls to serve steam heifers. Charlie Judd didn't know what the world was coming to.

Then, since Merton, there had been cavalry horses, gun-bullocks, screw-gun mules, commissariat camels, and elephants of the forty-pounder train — but pigs, never.

'Pineapples,' Dando resolved. He'd have a velveteen coat with contrasting plush lapels, set off with pearl buttons, a beaver-knapped top hat and a silk neck-cloth — a 'kingsman' — the coster's badge. His boots, as he recalled his father's, would be brightly polished, and stitched with hearts and flowers. He still remembered some of his father's tricks, of plumping out shrunken fruit, mixing dead eels with live, soaking nuts to increase their weight.

Given time, he'd take a woman. A judy could be an asset if she knew how to cure herrings, jelly eels and pickle salmon. But no pretty-faced, dainty thing, sod it. She'd need to be hard, with an unswerving loyalty, to stand at her man's side and fight with fists, boots and belt-buckle, and give as good as she got under the blanket. A pretty face made no difference in the dark, anyway. When a man poked the fire he didn't look at the bleedin' mantelpiece.

*

Sergeant Flynn had pushed his face to within inches of that of the young recruit in his stiff, new regimentals. 'Ye' walking days are over, see? In the Rifles ye don't walk. Ye don't even run. Ye bloody fly!'

And Joseph flew. At a hundred and forty paces to the minute, his leg muscles screamed for relief. His knees were torn and bloodied from incessantly flinging himself to kneeling fire, fingernails pulped from loading, ramming, and thumbing home the vital percussion cap. There was a raw, plum-black bruise on his shoulder from the butt of his Brunswick, and he dreaded the moment when he must peel off his sweat-clogged socks.

'HALT!' Flynn roared. He walked forward, hands behind back and chin lowered into a barrel chest. 'Is there any more of you Dandos at 'ome? Jes' in case the Ridgement needs 'em?'

'No, Sergeant.'

'A bleedin' pity.' Flynn shook his head, then surveyed the remainder of the half-company. 'A bleedin' pity. There's thirty-nine of yer what can't keep step.' He spun on ironshod heels, exploding. 'Only soddin' Dando! That's what schoolin' does for yer, see? One day 'e'll be an Hon'ry Lieutenant, passin' the port an' smokin' cigars.' The Sergeant paced slowly, confidently. 'An' Dando is so bleedin' superior ter the rest of yer, so dedicated ter the Ridgement, that 'ee wants extra drills when orl the other ignorant sods are swillin' beer in the canteen.' He paused. 'Two hours every night fer a week, wi' a forty-pound pack, great-coat an' rifle.'

Later, in the barrack-room, Meg Garvin — Corporal Garvin's wife — drained the blisters on his feet with a darning needle and length of worsted. 'They'll 'arden nicely in time, lad. If yer was a cavalry recruit, now, wi' two hours a night on a wooden 'orse, it'd be a bleedin' sight worse. I've seen 'em, walkin' like ruptured ducks.' She offered him a plug of black tobacco, extracted from between her bosoms. 'An' keep chewin' an' spittin'. There's Indians wot run 'undreds of miles, jes' chewin' an' spittin'. It sweetens yer juices an' fortifies yer liver.' She paused. 'An' I can always do wi' a drop o' neck-oil on payday — "London Pride", say. It's cheap an' cheerful. Or I never sez no ter a quart o' ale.'

But Joseph had already been bitten. On his first day Corporal Garvin had escorted him around Fort Pitt, to be thumbed by the surgeon, to sign his ten years' attestation, draw regimentals, rifle and bedding. On route, Garvin had pointed out the cook-houses, gymnasia, drill-ground, guard-house, finally halting at the door of the barracks canteen. He would, he offered, be delighted to show Dando the inside, and it was always his custom to welcome a recruit with a jug of beer, but unfortunately he — Garvin — had not a ha'penny in his pocket. Dando had one and sixpence. It was not a princely sum, Garvin agreed, but sufficient to purchase three quarts of Allsop's, most of which the Corporal despatched with speed and suitable apologies, while Joseph watched. It had been the first of many lessons, none of which was achieved without cost.

*

The four companies of the 60th were flung out in skirmishing order, waiting, their packs discarded and with swords fixed. Upwards of forty artillery pieces, both British and French, lurched and smoked as their sweating crews sponged, loaded and rammed, and the distant walls of Tang Ku were pocked with mushrooming explosions as the shots registered, vomiting splintered timber, stones and clods skyward. Through the haze of smoke and dust that shrouded the walls came the answering flashes of Chinese guns, this time ranged hopelessly high — but the horse of Sir John Michel, commanding the 1st Division, went down, kicking. The greying General rubbed ruefully at a bruised knee. 'Goddammit, those fellows are getting impertinent.' He nodded at an aide. 'You may signal the infantry to advance.'

A rocket soared, screaming, arching, then broke into twinkling stars high above their heads. The officers' glasses were out again, but this time searching the plain to their rear. Then someone said, 'Here they come, b'God. I'll lay fifty pounds to a penny this'll be the last time we'll see a British army advancing in line of columns with colours flying.'

It was a magnificent sight. In extended order, twenty-four guns were approaching at a gallop, the horses outstretched, lathering, the gun-wheels bouncing and the artillerymen clinging to their precarious seats on the bucketing caissons. Behind them, still distant, tramped the massed ranks of the infantry, with scarlet coats, bayonets fixed and standards curling — the Royals, the 31st and, on the right flank, the green-clad, rapid-marching remainder of the 60th.

The Indian yallers of the advance force stared in silence. After a dozen years in Bengal, where a man had to run, crawl on his belly, cling to cover, watch for the tell-tale flutter of a bird or the momentary flash of metal among rocks or shaded jungle, listen for the click of a gun-lock in the night darkness, they had never seen the ponderous drill formations of the Alma or Inkerman. Long ago, in Chatham, they had watched the Buffs and the Marines stamping and wheeling, all scarlet, brass and pipeclay, and had spat. They had learned since that the best soldier was one who shot faster and straighter than his enemy, and didn't get shot. Nobody had won a battle in India by marching up in review order with flags flying.

'Christ,' Dando mused. 'One battery wi' canister, an' two companies o' yallers, could shoot that bleedin' pantomime ter bleedin' bits.'

Holloran disagreed. 'Wid all thim brave bhoys, shure ye kin sleep safe in ye' bed o' nights, me ol' Dando.'

Joseph sniffed. 'I s'pose it's times like this when yer wishes yer could join up fer bleedin' ever, ain't it? Think o' orl them poor bastards at 'ome that ain't never 'eard the sweet music o' "Men under punishment", or tasted delicious salt beef an' peas, or 'ad a surgeon poke a stick up their arse, lookin' fer clap.'

On the far left the French infantry, already in line, were fixing bayonets. Major-General Michel turned to Colonel Palmer of the 60th. 'Do you suppose your greenjackets can reach that wall before the French, Colonel?'

'If they can't,' said Palmer, 'I'll have them double-marching for a month.'

'And if they can,' assured Michel, 'there'll be a double rum ration for every man. If de Montauban gets his blasted Tricolour up there first —' Palmer's whistle shrieked.

The four Rifle companies surged out of the entrenchment, the officers with pistols drawn. Behind them the guns had been joined by a rocket battery, which hurtled missiles over their heads in graceful, smoke-trailing curves. Underfoot, the ground was firm, and Dando thought of that other, similar occasion, three years before, with running feet rapping on a stone-hard maidan, the wide ditch and the great Kashmir Gate of Delhi ahead, and then, suddenly, the whole world turning to blood. He'd left Tom Brownlow and a piece of his skull on Delhi Ridge, and Surgeon Innes had sworn that, by rights, he should have been in the dead-house with the others. Someone had said that the Queen had ordered a medal struck for all the men of that murderous campaign, but they'd received nothing except a bounty of thirty-six rupees and ten annas. Dando had not even enjoyed the opportunity for a little honest looting.

With every available British and French gun pouring rapid fire at the Tang Ku walls, the Chinese reply was slackening. The approaching riflemen could see moving, gesticulating figures behind the battlements, hear gongs and rattles clashing, but when the Allied artillery suddenly fell silent to avoid dropping shot on the advancing troops, only a few gingalls blazed through the smoke, discharging wild balls in all directions. They couldn't hit a bleedin' barn at twenty paces, Dando spat, even if they stood on top of it.

It was here, sod it, just here at the edge of the ditch, that he'd caught the last one. It'd been the same, with Mr Heathcote hollerin' and cussin', smoke biting in the throat, an' bullets whining. Thank Christ these soddin' Chinamen weren't sepoys trained by British officers —

The sharpened stakes were hardly a hindrance, but the ditch was. It was deep, steeply banked, and filled with water of unknown depth. On their left the scrambling, red-trousered *poilus* had been similarly checked, but within minutes they would be joined by a following party of coolies with scaling ladders. Lieutenant Shaw cursed, then flung up an arm. 'The sluice gate!'

Fed from the Pei-ho, the ditch, at its junction with the river, was partially dammed, with the tidal interflow of water controlled by a heavy timber gate. At this point, too, the fort wall beyond sank into the muddy foreshore leaving, at low tide, a wide breach fenced only by a scattering of sagging stakes. San-Ko-Lin-Sin had planned not to fight in rain, or at low tide, but the foreigners were uncooperative.

There was a renewed frenzy of musket shots from the wall-top as Shaw, followed by Dando, Holloran, Sergeant Garvin, Rose and Bathurst flung themselves, slithering, over the gate. A gingall ball punched into the mud, feet away, drenching them with slime, but they were smashing aside the stakes now, swearing, panting up the sloping, debris-strewn foreshore.

A score of Chinese swarmed to meet them — squatfaced men, pigtailed, in quilted frocks and baggy trousers, armed with pikes and swords, screeching. The leader, a huge man with a red-plumed hat, ran at Shaw, but a bullet from the officer's Adam's pistol smashed him backwards. The next moment a second assailant clubbed Shaw to his knees, and Dando's sword-bayonet thrust viciously. 'Don't swaller the pips, yer yaller bastard,' he advised. Holloran whooped with the sheer delight of battle. 'Hould *thet*, ye murtherin' spalpeen! Hev ye niver heard ev Nuada ev the Bright Sworrd?' — his rifle-butt whirled, bone-smashing. 'Take *thet*, ye haythen divil!'

Resistance, however, was brief. As more and more riflemen clambered up the foreshore, trampling down the stakes, the Chinese were turning to run, or throwing down their weapons and shouting, '*Fang shen! Fang shen!*'

Shaw was on his feet, shaken but exuberant. 'We've licked the Frogs, dammit! They've not breached the gate yet! We've beat 'em!'

''Ave we come ter the right bleedin' war?' enquired Dando. ''Oo we s'posed ter be soddin' fightin'?'

Before them lay the interior of Tang Ku, the ground immediately inside the wall muddy, torn, and pooled with filthy water. Several artillery pieces, some with two barrels mounted on a single carriage, were surrounded by the bodies of Chinese, mutilated by shell splinters. Many had lengths of rope-like fusee tied to wrists — a fact that later had the London correspondents scribbling spitefully that Chinese gunners were tied to their guns to prevent them deserting their posts. Pyramids of roundshot, dangerously exposed baskets of powder, gun-pricks and a wide assortment of weapons were scattered everywhere.

Running, firing, stabbing, the four companies of the 60th herded an undisciplined mob of Chinese along the inner perimeter of the wall. As Holloran would mourn later, 'It wuz no foight et all, bedad. The auld goat in Letterkenny gave a divil more trouble.' Then, from ahead, came a burst of cheering. '*Vive la France! Vive l'Empereur! À Veking!*' There was a splintering crash of timber, the drum-beats of the *pas de charge*, and a French officer burst into view, sword waving, Tricolour held aloft, followed by a charging column of infantry. '*En avant!*' Confronted by the advancing Rifles, he halted, his face comical in its expression of surprise and disgust. '*Audace humaine! Sainte rage!*' Then he shrugged and spat into the mud. '*Eh, bien.*'

*

'The first two Frenchies inter Tang Ku,' said Sergeant Garvin, ''ave been promoted ter officers by General de Montauban. They reckons they was first in, 'corse they stuck up a flag, and we didn't.' The 60th Rifles was one of the few regiments of the British Army which, traditionally, possessed no regimental colours. Garvin looked at Dando and then Holloran, both of whom, with Lieutenant Shaw, had been the first to smash their way through the foreshore stakes. 'But if I was yew, I wouldn't be gettin' measured fer bleedin' officers' regimentals jes' yet, see?'

Dando, to whom the possibility had never remotely occurred, grinned. 'D'yer know somethin', Sar'nt? D'yer remember Flynn, at Chatham?' He sniffed. 'The bastard. 'Ee always said I'd be a soddin' officer. Superior, 'ee said, an' I'd be passin' the port an' smokin' bleedin' cigars. Breedin' will out, as Shakespeare said —'

'Gawd bleedin' 'elp us,' Garvin commented. 'If yew two was bleedin' officers, I'd transfer ter the fartin' Fire Brigade.'

'Ah,' Joseph returned, 'don't let bitterness rear its ugly, bleedin' 'ead, Sar'nt. 'Ave yer never 'eard the words o' the famous song —?' He began to sing to the tune of Officers' Mess call: 'Officers' wives 'ave puddin's an' pies, but sergeants' wives 'ave skilly. An' the rifleman's wife 'as nothin' at orl, ter fill 'er poor little belly.' He paused, then, 'Keats.'

Holloran nodded admiringly. 'The beauty ev it. Shure, St Michael an' his holy choir wid be struck soilent wid reverence.'

Dando, cleaning his Enfield with a scrap of oily rag, was thoughtful. 'No, men like us ain't the stuff fer officers, Irish — nor bleedin' want ter be. I've seen a few, promoted from the ranks, wiv no money 'cept their pay, which ain't near enough, an' starvin' ter pay their mess-bills. The toffs don't like 'em, and the ranks don't respect 'em. They can't afford dress regimentals, or even a ride in a soddin' cab, and they can't wed. They 'ave ter *prertend* they don't like cigars, or card-playin', or the opera, or ridin' ter 'ounds. An' they kin never afford another promotion. It's as worse as bleedin' gentlemen rankers, see? As out o' place as a fart in chapel.'

'Faith, an' ye're always roight, me ol' Dando,' marvelled Holloran. 'Whit wid the loiks ev you an' me be doin' in the Officers' Mess, wid silver plates an' toastin' the Quane ev'ry noight? An' nowhere ter spit, an' no puttin' ye' bloddy fingers in the salt, an' swate talkin' ter Lieutenant Shaw, an' all —'

'That reminds me,' Garvin interrupted. 'Dando — the Lieutenant's got yer on extra duty ternight.'

'*Agin?*' Dando snorted. 'Ain't 'ee never satisfied? Yer'd think 'ee might show a spark o' soddin' gratitude, wouldn't yer? If I 'adn't gutted that slant-eyed bastard this mornin', we'd be firin' three rounds o' blank over Lieutenant-bleedin'-Shaw's corpse!'

'It ain't much,' Garvin explained. 'Ye're ter go down ter the sluice gate, where we crossed, an' make sure it's shut an' bolted. If it ain't, an' there's a 'eavy tide, we could orl git flooded.' He paused. 'An' he was particular it 'ad ter be you.'

'I kin soddin' believe it!' Dando retorted. He made his way across the dusking Tartar cavalry paddock, strewn with abandoned saddles, spears, and broken banners. It would be dark in an hour, and scores of fires were glowing in the clay-built stoves left by the Chinese, boiling tea or peas, issue beef, or an occasional pig that had fallen victim to the earlier bombardment. The Pei-ho river was placid, ruddy from the setting sun, and showing not the slightest sign of flooding.

Disgruntled, Joseph lowered himself cautiously to the level of the heavy sluice gate. As he had anticipated, it was shut and firmly bolted. But there was something else he had not anticipated. On a narrow ledge, visible from only a few feet in the gloom, stood a bottle of brandy.

*

'As I was tellin' yer, before,' Dando lectured Holloran, 'yer kin never judge anyone *by looks*, see?' He took another mouthful and passed the bottle to his companion. 'Mark my words, Irish, that young man will *go far*, see? I sed it before, an' I'll say it agin —'

Holloran nodded contentedly. 'Faith, an' ye're always roight, me ol' Dando —'

10

Tien-tsin seethed with fear and speculation, with argument and disbelief. The province was no stranger to the ravages of armies, of rebellious war-lords, invading Mongols, brigands and river pirates. Armies had come, had burned and sacked, had departed or had been absorbed, and life had resumed. But now the incredible, the impossible, had happened. An army of foreign barbarians, *fan-kwei*, stood at the gates of Tien-tsin and threatened the Celestial City of Peking — the first time in the long history of the Middle Kingdom.

How had this happened? Had not the mighty San-Ko-Lin-Sin contemptuously reported that the barbarians had been massacred on the plain before Sinho? And what had happened to the impregnable Taku forts, which guarded the Pei-ho approaches?

For days, under a clear, hot sky, thousands of broken-spirited, dusty soldiers of the *luh-ying* had been streaming northward, watched apprehensively by the guards on the walls, some of whom, also, had deserted. There were other refugees, peasants, merchants, stooped and laden women, wailing children. Bullocks hauled cumbersome, solid-wheeled carts, loaded with chattels and livestock, intermingled with Tartar cavalrymen on their shaggy ponies, ill-humouredly lashing with their whips at any who impeded their passage. Old people sat wearily in the dust or dragged their thin legs under bamboo poles suspended with swaying bundles. The river was crowded with junks, sampans, and boats under oars, The barbarians, it was said, had great iron ships that ignored the vagaries of the wind, and had already shorn through three successive booms of chain and timber, smashing to matchwood every war-junk that had dared to oppose them.

P'u Sung Ling, Mandarin of the Plain Glass Button, was plagued with uncertainty. Several times each day he ordered his litter to the wall, where an increasingly truculent officer of the garrison pointed out the tents and guns of the barbarians on both sides of the river. Already speculating traders from Tien-tsin, having found the hairy ones not ill-disposed, were hawking ice, grapes, melons, beef and mutton. He had sent his groom, his *marfoo*, to ascertain the possibility of the foreigners' general accepting an indemnity in bullion, but the *marfoo* had not returned. Then several smoke-belching gunboats had anchored in mid-river. Red-coated soldiers had hoisted strange flags over the gate, where they now mounted guard.

Fung Yu-lan, the notary to the Council, advocated immediate flight. Soon — today or tomorrow — the barbarians would enter Tien-tsin in force, and then it would be too late. The great San-Ko-Lin-Sin himself had already been seen, with a small escort, hurrying northward towards the Celestial City, presumably intending to lead new armies against the *fan-kwei* invasion. It would be better to follow him, to safety. Tien-tsin was at the mercy of the foreign soldiers, which meant brutal vandalism, violence, rape, and thousands of dead. P'u Sung Ling, however, considered that San-Ko-Lin-Sin had received the dreaded summons to the Summer Palace, where he would grovel in shame at the feet of the Son of Heaven. In Peking there was no compassion for failures, and the headsman's sword was sharp and swift.

Even so, there was good reason for flight. He knew what happened to the people of a captured town, and foreign soldiers could be no different to Chinese. What could not be carried away would be smashed or burned. Hands, feet, noses, and women's breasts would be hacked off, children impaled on spears, old people ridden down. He, P'u Sung Ling, had a house of great value, precious porcelain, jades, coin, silks and tapestries, and when the barbarians overran Tien-tsin he would be defenceless. Fung Yu-lan was right in one respect. They must fly. He would have carts loaded with the most valuable of his goods, and they would follow the western bank of the Pei-ho to Peking — or San-Ko-Lin-Sin's army, whichever was nearer. He would also have several armed porters for protection against thieves, and he would take his senior wife and one or two others — but not all. Most must remain in Tien-tsin, to maintain the house against his return, just in case Fung Yu-lan was wrong. And he would leave money to keep the incense burning in the Temple of Kuan-ti.

P'u Sung Ling, as he accompanied his heavily laden carts northward, did not know that a junk on the river, passing in the opposite direction, carried envoys from the Summer Palace in Peking, seeking terms from the foreigners for a treaty of peace.

*

The Taku forts had proved far from impregnable, although their capture had not been quite as easy as Dando had predicted — 'like takin' cake orf a blind baby'. This time the Chinese made a spirited resistance, partly because the complexity of their defences made desertion difficult. The attack had opened at 5 in the morning with a barrage from eight heavy guns, three 8-inch mortars, both Armstrong batteries and the rocket battery, while the infantry waited. For some time the Chinese defenders maintained a counter-bombardment which, since it included two 32-pounders abandoned by the British during the previous year, could not be entirely ignored. But the Chinese' negligence in handling their explosives led to their first reverse. In quick succession, two magazines erupted with colossal explosions, and within minutes the fort's guns were silent.

The 44th and 67th Foot, and the French 102nd, trod forward, the leading assault parties reaching within thirty yards of the wall in the face of a punishing musketry fire. Progress across numerous wet-ditches was laborious and slow, further hampered by the accompaniment of several large and clumsy pontoons which proved useless for the purpose of crossing the narrow waterways. One of them was wrecked by a single heavy shot, the fifteen sappers carrying it flung, blood-spattered, into the mud, Sir Robert Napier had his glass struck from his hand by a matchlock bullet and his boot cut by a second, while his aide received a ball through his helmet and another in his thigh.

By an incredible effort, blaspheming artillerymen had hauled two howitzers across the ditches, to open fire at the gate at a range of only fifty yards. The gate was of massive timber, heavily ironbound, but the 8-inch round-shot splintered it from its lintel, and a mixed force of 44th and 67th raced towards it, cheering. Following several minutes of desperate hand-to-hand fighting, the breach was carried, with the Queen's colour of the 67th set up over the wall.

Mr Parkes had once said that, if the Chinese were cornered, they would fight like tigers. Today they fought, and later there would be Crimea veterans to swear they would rather face the Redan at Sevastopol than a fort of Taku. British losses were 17 killed and 184 wounded, the French roughly the same, and six Victoria Crosses were subsequently awarded for the day's action. Chinese dead lay everywhere, sprawled over guns, hung from their own stakes, outstretched and contorted in piles, mutilated, burned. When the fighting ceased, Signor Beato, an Italian photographer, scuttled excitedly from place to place, pleading with the soldiers to leave the corpses until he had set up his clumsy apparatus. '*Meraviglioso! Lo tenga un momento! Eccelente!*'

'Jes' the thing fer yer bleedin' mantelpiece, Irish,' Dando suggested. 'A pitcher wiv yer foot on a 'eadless Chinaman.'

'Shure, an' wid his jaws open,' Holloran agreed.

Soon after midday a boat under oars, and carrying a white flag, was observed crossing the Pei-ho from the direction of the remaining Taku forts. From it climbed two military mandarins, accompanied by an interpreter. The two officers were robed in buff grass-cloth, with waist-belts set with precious stones, and conical straw hats from which tassels of red horsehair hung. They had brought, they said, a despatch from the Governor-General of the province who, following the departure of San-Ko-Lin-Sin, had assumed responsibility for all Imperial forces in the area. In accordance with the courtesies common to all civilised nations, Governor Hung asked leave to surrender the remaining forts of the Taku group, and pleaded an armistice pending the arrival of envoys from Peking.

*

The road northward to Tien-tsin, laid with stone blocks but in bad repair, clung to the river. On both banks were wide fields of rice or millet, varied by occasional orchards, or pasture in which cattle browsed. As the European troops passed through riverside villages, the people gathered to chatter excitedly, seeming to have lost much of their earlier fear, although women still turned their faces away or ran to hide from the foreigners' evil eye. There was an abundance of foodstuffs offered for sale — poultry, fish, watermelons, apples, peaches and grapes. Itinerant piemen set up charcoal stoves at every halt, dogs barked, and urchins followed the columns for miles, seeking to carry baggage for a few cash.

Tien-tsin, they had been told, was one of the great cities of northern China, but any expectations of marble palaces and gilt-domed temples were rapidly dispelled on their arrival. True, Tien-tsin was larger, considerably larger, than Pehtang or Sinho, and it had an imposing gate flanked by high walls. In all other respects, however, it could only be described as a dirty little hole of a town — a complexity of narrow lanes, shabby houses of slate-coloured brick with windows of trellis covered with paper, open-fronted, cavernous shops and warehouses, muddy, stinking canals, with occasional open spaces in which vast mounds of salt were covered with ragged matting.

There were several pagodas and a few houses of better quality, surrounded by compounds. The streets were noisy with the clatter of wooden-soled feet, shouting traders with their ropes of coins, thronged with townspeople, lounging Imperial troops, dark and dirty priests, market stalls, carts, and litters on the shoulders of coolies. Everywhere was a pervading smell of rottenness, urine and smoking joss-sticks.

'It ain't so much the stink, see?' Dando said. 'It's the *sort* o' stink. Some stinks is orlright, others ain't.' He decided to expand on the subject. 'Things like beer an' baccy, f'instance, them's orlright — or liver an' onions, say. But take pigs, or camels, or O'Toole's socks —'

'Bedad, pigs es foin,' Holloran protested. 'Pigs es better than O'Toole's socks. Faith, the Divil himself widn't slape wid O'Toole's bloddy socks under the bed.'

'It's them long thin cheroots, stuck in pots,' Dando explained, referring to the smouldering joss-sticks seen everywhere. 'If that's wot Chinese shag's like, I ain't surprised they don't smoke it proper. It's worse'n bleedin' work'ouse snout.'

'Thet's the truth,' Holloran agreed.

'It's a bleedin' good job we 'ave our feet ter the pole, that's orl.' Dando glanced around. 'Wot we want is a bottle o' *samshu* —'

'An' no pickled turrds, bedad. Shrimps es foin, an' thim little bits o' pork mixed wid string, but not turrds —'

At that moment, from beyond a nearby, low wall, came a high-pitched, pleading cry of fear. The two men paused in their strolling, and would then have moved on, but the cry was repeated, tinged with terror, followed immediately by a male laugh. Mildly curious, they walked to the wall.

Beyond was a paved courtyard of several levels, fronting the entrance of a large house — the largest they had yet encountered in Tien-tsin. There were flowering shrubs, a dovecote and a rock pool with a miniature marble bridge, and Dando thought of the puzzling blue pattern he had once seen on a set of plates at the house of Colonel Finnis where he, Dando, had been a below-stairs domestic. Of more immediate interest, however, was that, on the stone stairs leading to the house, a man and a woman were struggling together.

They watched for several seconds. ‘’Ee’s after a bit o’ stink-finger,’ Dando decided. ‘But ’ee don’t ’ave to knock shit out of ’er, does ’ee?’

*

With the Master and old Mother Lightning gone from the house, the daily routine had lost much of its purpose. Yü still rose at dawn, to clean vegetables, sponge floors, feed the fowls, collect infants’ urine, feed the fire with fuel, and eat her bowl of scraps by the kitchen hearth, but if there was less purpose, there were more occasions for bruises and pulled hair. She was the least of the menials, and without the supervision of Tien Mu, she was slave to all. No longer content with cold water for washing, they must have hot, and dishes of tea at all hours. Dried fish was no longer adequate, but fresh had to be gutted. One wanted vegetables, another rice, a third cucumber or pumpkin. The concubines demanded their hair be combed and searched for vermin, when once they combed each other’s, and the pig coolie was drunk when two sows had farrowed, with nine piglets rolled on and dead — and Yü beaten for it.

But the weals on her arms were as nothing to the news that a barbarian army had reached the walls of Tien-tsin, and that most of the *luh-ying* had fled. Other female menials, who had visited the market by the gate, returned with excited, whispered reports of the foreigners. There were two kinds — ruddy-faced ones with blue eyes and whiskers under their ears, and brown-skinned ones with turbans, fine black beards and moustaches, the second seeming to be the slaves of the first, although they did not kowtow. The ruddyfaced ones were those with the evil eye, and on their first arrival dozens of women had jumped into the canal to escape their gaze, whereupon, incredibly, the barbarians had also jumped in to haul them, screaming, ashore. Such was an indication of the foreigners’ evil, for were not the women now assured of ill-fortune, of stillborn or girl children, of barren sows and non-laying fowls, spoiled cooking, and many beatings from husbands who would surely take other wives?

And there was still Kiaking, the strange one, who had not accompanied the Master’s party towards Peking, and for days had sulked in his chamber. Sometimes they could hear him talking to himself, the noise of furniture being thrown, or pottery smashed. Without Tien Mu, none dared to enter, but left food at the door, dreading the moment that he would emerge.

When he did emerge, the menials scattered, suddenly discovering they had urgent tasks in obscure parts of the house or grounds. Yü had no conveniently urgent task, but she hurried to the courtyard, from where she could retreat no further, and waited by the rock pool. She had gone into the streets of Tien-tsin only on rare occasions, and it was forbidden for her to do so alone.

Kiaking had trodden sullenly through the deserted rooms, with only an occasional glimpse of a frightened servant flying from his approach. When he reached the courtyard, his anger was simmering, and his eyes fastened on the trembling Yü.

There could be no Tien Mu to intervene this time. Two kitchen women peered nervously from behind the summerhouse, but she could expect no help from them. Indeed, if Kiaking vented his sadistic ill-humour on Yü, it was probable that the others would be spared. And the more violent he was, the more he would exhaust his lust. After all, she was only the commonest house menial, with ugly feet, and of no account.

Yü froze. Already she could feel vomit reaching for her throat, but she could not run. Kiaking grinned. 'I am going to beat you,' he said, 'until you bleed. When I have finished, you will crawl like an animal, begging for man-fruit. There is no stupid old woman to help you now. I am going to beat you as you have never been beaten before, and you will always remember. Whenever you see me, you will fall on your knees, whining like a heated bitch, and your tongue panting —'

*

''Ee don't 'ave ter knock shit out of 'er,' Dando repeated. 'They don't usually need more'n a couple o' clouts ter make 'em see reason.' The spectacle of a man beating a woman was something to be watched with interest but seldom interfered with. A man was fully justified in giving his woman the weight of his fist for several reasons, including laziness, disobedience or infidelity, and it was nobody else's concern.

'Faith, the divil's givin' her a bastin', an' no mistake,' Holloran agreed. 'She'll not be doin' ut again, whitever ut wuz.'

Dando frowned. 'She'll not be doin' anythin' at orl if 'ee don't bleedin' stop.'

‘Wimmin an’ dogs,’ Holloran shrugged, ‘shure, they both nayd a rig’lar bastin’ ter let thim know ye’re in charrge — but ef ye loik, I’ll give the Chinaman a mouthful ev teeth.’

Dando shook his head. ‘Yer’ve got ter try soddin’ diplomacy first, see? There’s such things as provokin’ international incidents. It’s orl written down somewhere, like QRs.’ He swung his legs over the low wall.

Crouched on the steps, Yü sobbed, burying her head in her arms and jolting as Kiaking kicked at her with wooden-soled boots, panting. Her loose tunic was shredded to her waist, her shoulders bruised and lacerated, and one eye blackened and closed. Wracked with pain, terrified, and with consciousness failing, she prayed for her beating to be finished, so that she could be compliant, to crawl like an animal, whining, begging for man-fruit.

Dando tapped Kiaking on the arm. ‘If I was you, matey, I’d bleedin’ chuck it, see? She’s ’ad a gutfuh!’

Kiaking whirled, his sweating face flushed, his eyes rolling. In almost the same movement his arm swung, and the flat of his hand lashed into Dando’s face.

‘Diplomacy, es ut?’ Holloran breathed, closing his eyes. ‘B’Jasus, there’s goin’ ter be *unmitigated slaughterr* —’

Few men of Queen Victoria’s Army would serve ten years without involvement in bloody battles with fists, boots and belt-buckles. Drunken brawls between men of different regiments were common, and rivalling commanding officers might consider the men’s bruises punishment enough if the regiment’s honour had been stoutly defended. Two men sharing a grudge would often meet *under* prize-ring rules, arranged by the officers and with heavy wagers placed on the outcome — there being a theory that fist-fighting enhanced prowess with the bayonet. The Army was no place for weaklings, no place for a man who would not fight until he was blind and deaf with blood and contusions, hands broken, wrists swollen like sponges, and helplessly reeling from shock and fatigue.

Every man cursed his own regiment as the worst in the Army, but let a man of another corps utter the merest word of criticism, and the result was blood-spattered carnage. To be hit in the face by a slant-eyed bastard of a Chinaman could have only one sequel.

And it was, as Holloran had predicted, unmitigated slaughter.

When Dando had finished, Kiaking was outstretched on the steps, drooling red slime and teeth, with both jaw and nose broken and grotesquely twisted, lips pulped, and eyes the merest slits in swollen blackness. Dando spat in the rock pool. '*Perliteness,*' he explained, 'don't cost yer bleedin' nuthin'.'

'Nuthin' et orl, me ol' Dando,' Holloran nodded from his seat on the wall. 'There's no nayd ter het a man jes' fer spaykin', bedad.' He transferred his attention to the prostrate Kiaking. 'Shure, he's restin' nice an' aisy. Tom Sawyer himself cudn't hev done ut wid more elegance.'

*

For the moment, both men had forgotten Yü. She had watched through splayed fingers the vicious punishing of Kiaking, and when it was finished she kept her gaze to the ground, not raising it above the dusty boots and green breeches of the barbarian, for fear of his evil eye, but it was a precaution that could not be sustained. When he turned to speak to his comrade at the wall, Yü pulled herself to her feet, painfully, wiping the blood from her own face.

What she saw was a short-statured man with black, close-cropped hair under an oddly-shaped hat. True, he had whiskers under his ears, but his face was not red, as she had been expecting. It was almost walnut. Furthermore, she realised with a jolt, his eyes were not blue, but brown. Was it not blue eyes that were evil? He was unbuttoning the collar of his green tunic, and she saw the sweat in the creases of his neck, which was not hairy.

Should she kowtow? It was said that the foreigners did not kowtow. Perhaps, Yü decided, she would first offer her thanks. She bowed three times, suppressing a wince. '*Hsieh hsieh.*'

His eyes were directed fully at her, and she felt her belly knot. Then, incredibly, he grinned. 'It's orlright, missie. When yer ol' man's finished spewin', yer can tell 'im it was the *Ruffel ka-Pultan*, wot eats bleedin' Chinamen fer breakfus'.' She did not understand a word, but his voice was good-humoured. 'An' yer'd better put a bit o' raw steak on that eye o' your'n. It looks like yer've jes' done fifteen roun's.' He turned to depart. '*Samshu,*' he told Holloran. 'I've got a mouth like the arse-end of a sewer.'

*

Two days previously they had located a *samshu* shop of which the proprietor spoke pidgin English, a polyglot vocabulary that the British troops had already begun to master. He welcomed them now, nodding and smiling. 'Halloa. No seea longa time.' It had been only two days. '*Samshu* velly number one good-ah. I sell 'em plum cash, alla same *cumsha*.'

Two bottle *samshu*.' Dando raised two fingers. 'Chop chop. Can do?'

'All same. Can do.'

Sitting cross-legged, they eyed lazily the busily passing traffic of the street beyond the door, their tunics unbuttoned and belts loosened. A pair of urchins peered at them curiously, shouted cheekily, and scampered away, laughing. Dando grinned, and then his expression froze. Standing at the door, with eyes demurely to the ground, was the Chinese woman whose thrashing he had just interrupted.

'Soddin' 'ell,' he frowned.

Yü walked forward apprehensively. '*Ming chiao Yü*.' She placed a hand on her chest. 'Yü.'

'Me?' He shook his head. 'Jus' now no wanchee anythin', see? No wanchee. Sometime, p'rhaps I come you, savvy?'

Holloran examined her. 'Dando, me jewel,' he observed, 'she's got rig'lation fate, an' orl. Wid ye be supposin' —?'

'No, I bleedin' wudn't. Besides, she looks like she's been 'it by a runaway gun limber.'

The proprietor had returned, trotting, with bottles and cups. Seeing Yü, he shouted at her angrily, waving her away. She addressed herself to Dando again, determinedly. '*Wo ken hsien-sheng ch'u*.'

Dando uncorked a bottle. 'Solly. No can. Tomollow.' Yü appealed to the proprietor with a stream of unintelligible Chinese. The man listened, his face perplexing. When she had finished, he turned to Dando.

'Bad joss, plenty. Cow chillo say no jig-jig. Cow chillo say belonga you, alla same slave, heya?'

'Alla same wot?'

'Slave. Cow chillo belonga you. Ten year, twenty year, savvy? What for hit mass 'er, bam-bam, heya? Chinee custom, plenty longa time. You save life, life belonga you. Savvy?'

Dando snorted. 'She kin kiss my soddin' —' He stopped. 'Tell her no can. Solly. Alla same no wanchee slave, no wanchee jig-jig. Finish.'

The proprietor was adamant. 'No can.' He shook his head gravely. 'Too muchee bad joss. Cow chillo folloa, day, night, alla same. No can house, no wanchee one piecee cow chillo. Velly bad, come you. Can?'

'Did I iver tell ye, me ol' Dando,' enquired Holloran, 'ev the time I won the leg ev porrk, cloimbing the grasy pole in Strabane — ?'

'I ain't won bleedin' nuthin' yet,' Dando retorted. He returned to the Chinese. 'Tellum no can. How muchee cash wanchee no can, alla same?' A few coppers, and likely the woman would disappear.

The man shook his head again. 'No squeeze, savvy? Cow chillo die first, belonga you, ten year, twenty year —'

Holloran was conciliatory. 'Faith, an' ye shud count ye' blessin's. Where else wid they give ye wimmin ter kape, bedad, jes' fer hettin' a man senseless?'

'In that case,' Dando pointed out, 'them six bleedin' wimmin orf the floatin' whore-shop are orl your'n — *an'* the Mother Judger. I wudn't be surprised if they ain't steerin' up the soddin' Pei-ho now, lookin' fer yer.'

Holloran considered the possibility carefully. 'The diabolical haythens! The injushtis ev it! Where else in the bloddy worrld wid ye find yeself wid a *haraym* ev slant-eyed, yaller wimmin — jes' fer breakin' a man's jaw?' He choked. 'Shure, they'd niver belayve lit in Letterkenny ef I swore ut on me knays!'

Both men took fortifying mouthfuls of *samshu.* Yü waited by the door. In her estimation she had absolutely no choice. It was firmly understood that if a man saved a life, he possessed that life thereafter. No Chinese would rescue another from death if he could avoid doing so; the responsibility that followed was too daunting. And there was no doubt in Yü's mind that the foreigner had saved her from death. Kiaking, in his evil frenzy, would have continued to batter her until she was a broken corpse to be thrown in the river. That there might be complications in being possessed by a foreign barbarian she did not doubt, but the situation was not of her choosing, nor could she change it.

She kept her gaze, correctly, to the floor, but presently she raised it surreptitiously to examine her new lord. His nose was not excessively big, and she was glad that his face was not red. True, he had no pigtail, and under his clothes he was undoubtedly covered with hair. All barbarians were. From the distance at which she stood, she could not smell him. Did he already have a number-one wife?

Dando and Holloran were becoming increasingly fortified. 'It ain't no good, see?' Dando told Yü. 'No can, savvy? You belonga bull chillo, Chinee — not soddin' Rifleman Dando. No wanchee jig-jig. You pissey-orf, play mah-jong, heya? No wanchee, savvy?'

Yü bowed. '*Wo yeh ch'u.*' Her new lord was masterful, which was good, and his side-whiskers rose and fell as he spoke.

'The black-hearted haythens,' Holloran breathed, visualising a flower-painted junk anchored off Tien-tsin. 'Whit wud a man do wid *six* slant-eyed bloddy wimmin, bedad?'

'Keep 'em under the bleedin' bed,' Dando offered, 'wiv the pigs.'

Holloran pondered on the suggestion, but rejected it. 'Shure, there wudn't be the space, wid the praties an' orl.'

'Six,' Dando mused, his comprehension becoming a little fuddled. 'That still gives yer a day orf on Sundays — unless, o' course' — he frowned — 'ol' Mother Judger still wanted 'er conjugal rights. Then bang goes yer bleedin' day orf.'

Holloran winced. 'B'Jasus.'

Beyond the door the daylight was fading. 'It'll be Retreat in arf 'our,' Dando said. They buttoned their tunics and rose. Yü, who had stood unmoving for an hour, her hands clasped across her middle, raised her bruised face. Dando drew a deep breath, then fumbled in a pocket for a few small coins. ''Ere — buy yourself a pie, then go an' tell yer ol' man it weren't your soddin' fault, see? Anyway, 'ee ain't goin' ter do nothin' ternight except sleep it orf.' They passed into the street, leaving Yü staring blankly at the coins in her hand.

It was early September, uncomfortably sultry despite the approach of evening. The 60th's lines of bell tents stood on the grassy plain to the eastward of Tien-tsin, surrounding the monastery of Hai-kwang, occupied by the Commissariat Department. At the erratic approach of Dando and Holloran, the picquet was herding the last of the Chinese hawkers from the lines, and in a few minutes Tattoo would be beating. In front of the officers' mess-tent, the band was playing 'The Old Folks at Home'.

'Shure, an' it's es swate es the harp ev Cú Chulainn.' Holloran hiccoughed. 'Hev ye niver heard ev Cú Chulainn, me ol' Dando? Theer wuz a man fer ye. He cud turrn around in his skin so's his fate an' knees wuz ter the back, an' his arrse ter the front. Theer wuz fire spurrting from his mouth, an' a jet ev black blood from the top ev his head —'

'When I larst knew 'im,' Dando remembered, ''ee was called Sergeant Flynn.'

Rifleman Wilson was polishing his boots with a mixture of saliva and black-ball when they entered the tent. 'Orders is up,' he told them. 'We march tomorrer morning, fer Poo-kow. Field order, sixty rounds, an' three days' rations.'

'Poo-kow?' grimaced Dando. 'I kin guess wot sort o' stink that'll be.'

'Yer ain't 'eard about the Marines,' Wilson went on. 'It was some o' the Jollies wot jumped in the Yu-ho Canal ter pull out them Chinee wimmin. Now they can't git rid of the bleeders. The wimmin. They sez they *belong* ter the men wot saved 'em, an' the Jollies 'ad ter double their picquets ter keep 'em out o' the lines.' He spat on the toe of a boot. 'Would yer believe it? Fancy 'aving ter *fight* wimmin *orf*!'

'The Divil!' Holloran gaped. He lifted the tent flap cautiously and peered towards the distant Pei-ho. There was no sign of a junk painted with flowers. 'It's a murtherous bloddy place, so 'tis, where a man can't slape paceful in his tint wid'out sintries ter kape him from bein' a victim o' scarrlet wimmin —!'

*

But Holloran had not looked in the direction of the 60th's guard-tent, a hundred yards away. Had he done so, he might have observed the shape of a lone woman in the dusk beyond the pacing guard. She stood motionless, eyeing the soldier as he tramped, halted, and tramped again. She did not believe that he was her lord, but could not be entirely sure. They all looked so alike. The sentry had his shako strapped firmly under his chin, and the one thing she clearly remembered about her lord was that he had a wide, white scar on the side of his head, only partially hidden by his black hair.

When Dando and Holloran had left the *samshu* shop, Yü had followed. It was right that she should walk several yards behind. The two men had weaved an uncertain passage through the Street of Everlasting Prosperity, then clattered over the thronged boat-bridge spanning the Yu-ho Canal. It was then that Yü became aware of the swelling stream of foreigners, all returning to their camps — some green-clad, some in scarlet, and the strange, brown-skinned ones, bearded, in blue tunics and white breeches. There were cavalrymen in white solar helmets, straw-hatted sailors from the gunboats in the river, and coolies of the Labour Corps. It was all very confusing, and becoming increasingly difficult to keep in sight the two men she followed, or even identify them. She broke into a trot, but it was too late. Suddenly there was a big tent, and a man with a gun. 'That's as far as yer kin go, missie. No natives after Tattoo, an' no wimmin at any time. Cow chillo no can. Too many piecee sodgers, savvy?' He winked. 'I git relieved at midnight, see? Jig-jig? If yer wants ter 'ang around — ?'

Yü had not understood a word, but she perceived that she could go no further. She waited. Beyond the guard-tent were long lines of other tents, with many men walking between them. Somewhere a band was playing soft music. Presently, as dusk fell, the music ceased, and gradually the men disappeared into the tents. Then the liquid notes of a bugle floated on the air, and she observed that the sentry stood stiffly still. After that, there was silence, unbroken.

Yü had not eaten since early morning, but she was no stranger to an emptiness in her belly, and she possessed all the fatalistic patience of her race. Doubtless the foreigners had different customs to those of her own people, and she might have anticipated that women did not share the quarters of their masters. There were many things to learn — in particular the language that her lord and the *samshu* shop proprietor had spoken, of which she recognised occasional words. It was important that she understood her master's commands. There were so many things to be learned. Did he prefer green tea or black, his *dim sum* fried or steamed? And did he wish for infants' urine?

The moon was rising and, her legs tiring, she sat on her haunches.

11

With the forts of Taku captured, San-Ko-Lin-Sin defeated, Tien-tsin occupied, and the barbarian army moving remorselessly, unopposed, towards the Celestial City, there was consternation in the capital. Two weeks earlier, Lord Elgin, leader of the Anglo-French diplomatic mission, had outlined the Allies' terms to the first Chinese envoys — an apology and indemnity for the British and French losses of the previous year, ratification of the Treaty of Tien-tsin, the advance of the Allied forces to T'ungchow, only ten miles from Peking, and ambassadorial access to the Emperor.

The Chinese envoys had bowed and smiled, after their fashion, willing to agree to any demands that would halt the barbarians' all-devouring advance, even temporarily. Yes, they nodded, hostilities could cease and all would be well. The Son of Heaven, in Peking, would himself confirm it.

Lord Elgin and his ministerial colleagues — including Mr Parkes, the Commissioner of Canton, who should have known better — decided that the campaign was over. It required only diplomacy to finish what bayonets had begun. Equally convinced, General de Montauban ordered new sashes to be issued to the French detachments selected for escorting the ambassadors to Peking. Given luck and a good troopship, there was even a possibility of returning to Europe by Christmas.

Only General Sir Hope Grant was sceptical. He doubted the authority of the mandarins, who had hastened from Peking after the capture of the Taku forts, to make such wide-sweeping assurances. They had shown all the signs of men willing to agree to anything, simply to gain time. The Chinese, he knew, entertained an irrational compulsion to save face at all costs, a factor that influenced all negotiations, large or small. Grant, during his years of campaigning, had acquired the facility to think in his adversary's terms, to question motives, and to look for the snare. The mental processes of the Chinese were not compatible with those of Europeans, and Grant had a nagging suspicion that something was not quite right. He had no intention of withdrawing any of his force towards the coast in preparation for re-embarkation, and Christmas could wait for another year. When he saw the ratified treaty bearing the Emperor's joss, and a British ambassador established in Peking, his task would be completed, but not before.

As the days passed with the Chinese still apparently debating the peace terms, and no news available, Grant's opinions were gaining credence. By leisurely stages the troops followed the twisting Pei-ho, in the direction of T'ungchow, as the treaty had proposed.

And Peking, similarly, had no intention of agreeing to any terms imposed by foreigners until all possible evasive tactics had been exhausted. Winter was approaching, when campaigning would be difficult, if not impossible, and the foreign soldiers would want to go home. Weeks, perhaps months, of sterile discussions would wear down the Europeans' determination, and eventually they might settle for less, from sheer frustration. Alternatively, as the period of truce lengthened, the occupying forces would be lulled into a sense of complacency, exacerbated by inactivity and boredom. They were still grossly outnumbered, and scores of thousands of fresh Chinese troops were being hurried to the vicinity of Peking. There might well be an opportunity, truce or no truce, of surprising the foreigners and destroying them.

General San-Ko-Lin-Sin, whom the British referred to as Sam Collinson, and rumoured was a renegade Irish deserter from the Royal Marines, had not parted with his head in Peking. He was still the most experienced of the Chinese generals, and his reputation had survived the reverses suffered in the Taku area. He had, after all, butchered countless thousands of the foreigners before falling back on Peking with a mere two hundred cavalrymen.

It was San, now, who commanded the new army massing to the south-east of the Celestial City, and San had a plan. It was based on treachery, and could not possibly fail. In case it did fail, however, he did not want the Emperor near at hand to witness his embarrassment and thus make impossible his subsequent claims of glorious victory. In one of the many pavilions of the Summer Palace — that of the Fragrant Concubine — San-Ko-Lin-Sin respectfully argued that the Son of Heaven should demonstrate to the people his lack of alarm towards the situation by making a leisurely hunting tour of the remote North. Other members of the Grand Council disagreed. Such an action would only be interpreted as flight, they said, and a thousand years would not erase the shame of it.

The Emperor compromised. He would issue a Vermilion Decree stating that he, the Son of Heaven, was to leave Peking to assume personal control of the Chinese armies in the field, and thus assure a victorious conclusion to the war against the barbarians. In reality, however, he would undertake a hunting tour in the far North.

*

The faded green column of riflemen, with rifles slung and shoulders hunched under packs, swung on to the road towards Poo-kow, twelve miles distant. As far as the eye could see were fields of tall millet, interrupted only by occasional watch-towers and brick-kilns. The river on their right was hidden from view by a high flood-dyke, so that there was little to divert attention from a monotonous landscape except the constant flutter of birds — pied woodpeckers, tiny flycatchers, buntings, finches, wagtails.

The French were to follow one day behind, a welcome arrangement from the British viewpoint since, when the French led, they systematically appropriated everything of value, including fodder and fuel, slaughtered every pig, fowl and goat within reach, and left every camping site bereft of the smallest amenity. Even so, the commissariat was experiencing difficulty in feeding the Sikhs, who would not eat pork — the meat most easily available. There were insufficient fowls, and the long, arduous route from Pehtang, on the coast, was severely testing the supply wagons striving to keep pace with the advancing infantry, while the river was too low and hazardous for all but the smallest craft. It was also suspected that Chinese agents had been threatening the coolies of the Labour Corps. Many had deserted, some taking their pack-animals despite the vigilance of their escorts. It wasn't so much the salt beef and peas, as Dando complained. It was the bleedin' rum.

The column halted at the Temple of the Peach-flower — *Taou-hwa-she* — in the courtyard of which stood green-glazed dragons with bulbous eyes and fanged mouths, and tiny glass bells, suspended from the trees, tinkled with every breeze. Under moss-covered eaves a small wayside shop offered tea and wheat-cakes, and pigeons strutted, cooing.

'These Chinamen ain't got much idea o' runnin' a business,' Dando said. 'Tea an' cakes ain't no soddin' good, see? Wot they want is booze, an' entertainment, like the Eagle in the City Road, say — dancin' wimmin an' talkin' parrots, oysters, comical dogs, an' there was a nigger wot ate bleedin' fire an' broken glass.'

'Loik the ol' Phaynix on St Patrick's noight,' Holloran recalled nostalgically. 'Bedad, the Jackeens come out ev church, crossin' thimselves an' drippin' wid holy medals, ready ter foight anyone es soon es they've had a drop ev the stuff. Sackville Street's filled wid dhrunks an' polis' an' scraychin' Jezebels, wid fists flyin' and the blodd spurrtin', an' iveryone havin' the toim ev their loives —!'

'Bleedin' ecstatic,' Dando sniffed. 'I ain't surprised there's so many Irish fightin' Chinamen an' Paythans — jes' fer soddin' peace an' quiet.'

Holloran was peering fixedly at the road to the rear of the halted column. He drew a deep breath. 'Dando, me jewel, there's somethin' ye shud be knowin'. Wid ye be rememberin' thet little faymale wid the reglashun fate, in the *samshu* shop —?'

Dando stared at his companion for a long, painful moment, then slowly, very slowly, turned his head. On the road, twenty yards away, stood Yü.

'Well, I'll be a gun-bullock's bleedin' uncle!' Dando's eyes widened. 'Wud yer soddin' *believe* it? I arst yer, wud yer soddin' *believe* it?'

'Did I iver tell ye, me ol' Dando, ev the time I tuk a goat orl the way ter Ballymore market — sivinteen miles, so ut wuz. An' the next bloddy mornin', whit d'ye suppose wuz standin' outside the door, grinnin' loik the Divil —?'

'Ain't she got a bleedin' 'ome?' Dando asked.

Yü's feet clack-clacked on the uneven stones of the road as she trotted towards him. She bowed three times, her tired face smiling. '*Wo ken hsien-sheng ch'u.*'

'Soddin' arse-'oles,' Dando breathed. 'No can. Savvy? No wimmin in bivouacs, see? No cow chillo, no jig-jig. Yer'll git me seven days o' Number One. Why don't yer jes' bleedin' go 'ome?'

Yü frowned, concentrating. 'Me Yü, cow chillo, come you, alla same. Can?' She smiled again, proudly.

'It jes' ain't bleedin' justice, is it?' Dando whispered. 'Wot 'appened ter that soddin' junk, painted wi' flowers? *Six* o' the bleeders. *An'* Mother Judger.'

Holloran was unsympathetic. 'Shure, an' et's the auld law ev supply an' demand, me darlint. Are ye supposin' thet six hot wimmin wid want ter share one man, bedad? — an' wid me bein' bloddy near dead after only one? B'Jasus, didn't they be seein' they'd be six bloddy widders in a fortnight?'

Yü nodded vigorously. '*Ting la! Hao!*'

'Knock out yer pipes an' git fell in!' The sergeants were reforming the column, and the riflemen were climbing to their feet, shrugging their packs higher on their backs — the 'Devil's monkey' that clung to a man's shoulders with satanic tenacity, growing heavier with every jolting mile until muscles burned with aching. 'There yar,' Dando said. 'Yer'd better start walkin' back ter Tien-tsin.' He pointed southward. 'Tien-tsin, savvy? No can Poo-kow. Too muchee longa way, heya?'

She knew what he meant, and in that moment he saw the new-born confidence fade from her eyes. Although she had washed the blood from her face, she still showed the marks of her cruel beating from Kiaking, and now her shoulders drooped, her gaze that of a whipped animal. She ran a tongue over swollen lips, and waited.

'Gawd strewth!' Dando shook his head, frustrated. Then he heaved a breath. 'Yer look bleedin' famished. There's less on yer than a streak o' spit. When did yer lars' eat?' He did not wait for an answer. In the road the company was jostling into line, and in a few seconds Garvin would be bawling for him to move his arse. He thrust a hand into his haversack and withdrew his day's ration of hardtack — a fist-sized piece of salt beef — and some biscuit. ''Ere, fer Chris' sake, stuff that in yer belly-'ole, an' then piddle orf. This ain't the Society fer the Relief o' Destitute Young Persons —'

*

The orphanage and ragged school of the Society for the Relief of Destitute Young Persons had stood in the Borough Road behind a high wall crowned by imbedded, broken glass. The wall was not intended to keep intruders out; the building's gaunt appearance suggested little that was desirable to the most desperate of humans. Its brickwork was corroded by a century of London grime, streaked with water, the curtainless windows filthily opaque. Adjacent was the reeking premises of George Bell, disposer of refuse and purveyor of rags, firewood and bottles. The Borough Road, flanked by dirty little shops and costermongers' stalls, was heavily dung-scattered, for few here would pay a sweeper a ha'penny to clear a crossing through the constant droppings of carts, four-wheeled growlers, and Shillibeer's omnibuses.

Inside, the Society's building was stone-floored and damply cold. Mr Luker flexed his cane, or picked fragments of his breakfast from his teeth with dirty fingers. The orphans did not enjoy the privilege of breakfast, but waited until noon for potatoes, with bread purchased cheaply because of its staleness. At night there would be turnip soup, or thin skilly that retained a smell of mustiness from the years its constituent oatmeal had lain in some rat-infested warehouse. If orphans had to be fed, they did not have to be gluttons at public expense.

In addition to food, a roof and a blanket, the benevolent Society provided education — Scripture, Arithmetic, and Reading. Joseph Dando, at six, was indifferent towards the first because he was never entirely certain whom Lord God was, finally deciding that, in view of the title, he must be a member of the nebulous Board of Governors. Arithmetic he detested because of its utter illogicality and, anyway, anyone with ten fingers did not need Arithmetic. Reading, however, was different. He conceded that there might be numerous occasions on which Reading would be very useful. He would be able, for instance, to study, with mouth-watering anticipation, the gourmandising delights of a workman's ordinary bill of fare, discerning the availability of mutton pie, pig trotters, and suet pudding. There were playbills outside music-halls simply crammed with exciting words — if the illustrations could be believed — about duels to the death, stabbings and shootings, and of course there were always books, although Joseph did not think that he would ever aspire to reading a book. There was nothing to gain by it.

In later years, Joseph Dando would forget the thrashings from a sadistic Mr Luker, the bitter cold of winter, the stench of the shit-pit and the refuse yard in summer, and he would scarcely recall a name or a face of any of his childhood companions. He would forget the condescending visitors and their fat, contemptuous children, and the annual departures of bands of excited waifs to the near-slavery of apprenticeships in the industrial North. But he would never forget hunger — persistent aching hunger — or the rapture he experienced at the sight of an extra tater on his plate. For the rest of his life he would recognise hunger in others, and could no more refrain from offering relief than he could have stopped breathing. He was not being charitable, and would have mouthed an obscenity at the suggestion. It was just that nobody 'ad ter be bleedin' 'ungry if some other bastard 'ad soddin' grub, see?

*

Poo-kow was a replica of a half dozen previous riverside villages, with the women running for the security of their scattered, thatched houses at the soldiers' approach. A water-wheel, kept in motion by a plodding, scimitar-horned ox, scooped water from the river to irrigate orchards of pears and apples, and there were two watch-towers, like ships' masts with crows' nests, to survey the road in both directions. Fowls scratched, dogs barked, and black, low-bellied pigs rooted among heaped garbage, swarming with flies. A deputation of senior villagers, having hastily donned their best clothes, bowed and smiled, chattering meaningless Chinese at the tired and dusty riflemen.

Within a few minutes the field kitchens were smoking, and Major Rigaud with several other officers were grouped together, discussing in low, irritable voices the news from Tien-tsin that had overtaken them. The Grand Council in Peking, it seemed, had refuted the terms of Taku. The mandarins accepting them had held no authority to do so. The truce would continue to be observed, but the Council needed more time. Would the European soldiers abstain from advancing farther? Or, at least, would they come no further than Ho-se-wu, thirty miles from Peking?

The news was annoying, and ominous. There were also reports of increasing concentrations of Chinese troops further up-river, in numbers that could scarcely be reconciled with the Chinese' declared intention of negotiating a peaceful settlement. Why should the Chinese be massing troops in the path of the Allies other than for a resumption of hostilities? Could there be a sinister motive behind the plea for delay?

Neither Dando nor Holloran would have been unduly concerned about the machinations and frustrations of diplomats, even were they aware of them. They had heard of Lord Elgin and his French counterpart, Baron Gros, and had a vague understanding of their function which, however, they did not consider particularly relevant to a military campaign. There was only one real way of settling a dispute, and that was with bayonets. One side won — usually the British — and the other side lost. That was that. The civilian diplomats, with their black frock coats and watch-chains, signed a piece of paper, and were knighted for it. Then the soldiers were ordered somewhere else, to fight another campaign, so that some other frock-coated civilian could be knighted. It was probably, as Dando would suggest, all written down somewhere, like QRs. At the moment, however, Dando had a more immediate problem.

'It's like 'aving a 'ooman shadder, ain't it?' At the roadside, ten yards away, Yü sat on her heels, her placid gaze never leaving him. 'It was a bleedin' mistake, giving 'er grub, see? Don't never give grub ter a stray. Don't never give soddin' nuthin'.' He spat. 'She thinks she *belongs*. Wot the bleedin' 'ell am I supposed ter do?'

'If she wants ter foller the drum,' Sergeant Garvin ruled, 'it's 'er democratic right, so long as she ain't hawkin' 'er piece in the lines. That's agains' reglashuns.'

'Shure, an' ye cud kick her en the tayth,' Holloran said, without conviction, then relented. 'Bedad, ye can't kick her en the tayth.'

'It's a public road, ain't it?' asked Edwin Wilson. 'Anyone kin walk where they soddin' like, on a public road. It's the Queen's bleedin' 'Ighway, see?'

'It ain't the Queen's 'Ighway,' Moss Rose contributed. 'It's the Emperor o' China's soddin' 'Ighway.'

'It's the Queen's 'Ighway by right o' conquest, see?' Edwin Wilson argued. 'We're 'ere, ain't we? An' the soddin' Chinese ain't.'

Dando snorted. 'It don't matter a monkey's fart 'oo's bleedin' 'ighway it is. Wot the soddin' 'ell am I supposed ter do?'

Nobody seemed anxious to volunteer advice. 'Shure,' Holloran agreed, 'et's an unspaykable responshibility, so 'tis.' Indeed, he considered, but for the grace of St Michael and all his angels, he might himself have been in the same predicament, only six times worse. It was a heavenly mercy, bedad, that the Pei-ho at Poo-kow was too shallow and weed-fouled for the passage of a junk painted with flowers. 'Did I iver finish tellin' ye, me ol' Dando,' he went on, 'ev the toim I tuk the auld goat ter Ballymore market? Sivinteen miles, ef ut wuz a yarrd — an' the next mornin', shure, there he wuz, grinnin' loik the Divil —'

'Bleedin' arse-'oles,' Dando breathed, 'wot's that got ter do wiv a soddin' Chinese woman that's stickin' ter yer like shit ter a blanket —?'

But Moss Rose was intrigued. 'Wot 'appened ter the goat?'

'Faith, an' he wuzn't grinnin' fer bloddy long, I kin tell ye. He moight hev saved himself the walk. Before ye cud spit, bedad, he wuz gutted, drained an' dishmembered.' He paused. 'Ef ye iver want an auld goat gutted, drained an' dishmembered —?'

"Every bleedin' day,' Dando heaved. There should be one in every soddin' 'ome.'

Holloran pondered. "Faith, not *ivery* day. Goat's orlright, but not ivery bloddy day.' He pointed a finger. "Wid I be tellin' ye, me ol' Dando, the foinest way ter cook auld goat —?'

'No, yer bleedin' wudn't. But if yer kin tell me the *foinest* way ter git rid of a Chinee woman —'

Jamie Bathurst lifted his shako to scratch his head, then grinned. "If yer axed the Colonel's permission ter marry 'er, yer cud take 'er on the strength, see? She'd git rations.'

'An' a blanket,' Holloran added. 'Orl wives on the strength gets rations an' a blanket.'

'There's times,' Dando gritted, "when a man sees the other bleedin' side of 'ooman nacher.'

Moss Rose was giving thought to the suggestion. "There's more in it than meets the eye, see? She cud cook, an' dob out the grub, do mendin' an' dhobeying, an' git paid from our stoppages — which kin be your booze money, 'corse wimmin don't need it.' He paused. 'Yer don't 'ave ter marry 'er *proper*, see? Jes' the Chinee way. Then, when it's time ter leave, yer give 'er a pat on the 'ead, and 'ooks it.'

'That's right,' Edwin Wilson agreed. 'An' if yer share the booze money, it means we orl git our mendin' an' dhobeying fer nuthin'.'

'An' free booze,' Holloran nodded.

Dando stared at his companions with a mixture of amazement and indignation. 'Yer kin orl git festered,' he retorted. 'If I 'ad a woman wot earned booze money, it'd be *my* bleedin' booze money, see?' He frowned. There just might, as Moss Rose said, be more in the suggestion than met the eye. It was at least worth thinking about.

'There ain't nuthin' in QRs,' considered Sergeant Garvin, 'about marryin' Chinee wimmin. There was men wot married *karanies* in India, but they was Queen's subjects. Mind, if it weren't a *proper* marriage —'

'If it weren't a *proper* marriage,' Moss Rose pointed out, 'yer cud share 'er around. When yer was on night picquet, fr'instance —'

'An' we orl git a free jig,' Holloran concluded. 'But only one a noight, bedad. Et wudn't be bloddy sanitray fer more thin one a noight.'

'Yer kin kiss my carrot!' Dando spat. 'Nobody is 'aving a jig, see? An' orl the booze money is *mine*, see? It's me wot wud be doin' the marryin', an' there's things wot's bleedin' sacred.' The more he thought about it, the more did lucrative horizons reveal themselves. It was odd that he had not thought of it before. There must be pitfalls, he imagined, but for the moment he could not see them. Sailors did it all the time, didn't they? He shot a glance at the road. Yü still sat on her heels, watching him. ''Oly matrimony ain't ter be entered in ter lightly, see? An' I ain't decided yet.' He sniffed, possessively. 'In the meanwhile, she's got ter be bleedin' fed an' watered.'

*

Yü had spent the little cash that Dando had given her on three joss-sticks to burn before the daughter of the Emperor of the Eastern Peak, Princess of Streaked Clouds, Pi-hsia-yüan-chün, who watched over women. Nobody else had concern for women. Yü wished she had been able to afford five joss-sticks, for all things human and spiritual were numbered in fives. There were five elements: wood, fire, earth, metal and water, five directions, five planets, five seasons, five times of day, five colours, five kinds of taste, five human relationships — father to son, man to woman, older to younger brother, prince to official, friend to friend. But perhaps Princess of Streaked Clouds would accept the humble three joss-sticks that accompanied her prayer for a life of utmost happiness with her new lord, and that she should please him.

Yü's expectations towards her future, both immediate and distant, were vague. She was unable to predict the foreigners' intentions and, even if they had been explained to her, she would not have understood them. Had her lord and his companions come to stay? The road led to Peking, but she had never been to Peking. Would they live in Peking? Alternatively, if they intended to depart, what was the foreigners' country like? Undoubtedly there would be women, presumably all looking exactly alike, with whiskers under their ears. Were the foreigners corn-growers, like the northern people, or rice-eaters like the Cantonese?

She was content that her lord had acknowledged his possession of her by giving her food. It had been strange food, but she knew she must be prepared for strange things. In time she would prepare and cook his food, and she was grateful that she had learned much in the kitchen of P'u Sung Ling. Now would she reap the benefit of the years under the stern eyes of old Mother Lightning, and there was little she could not do.

It was only her feet. Her new lord had pretended not to notice her ugly feet, perhaps to save his face. She recognised that it must be embarrassing for a man to refer to such an impediment in his woman-slave. She resolved that if she ever unworthily bore her lord a female child, she would bind its feet more tightly than any she had seen, and so minimise her lord's further embarrassment. But she would burn more joss-sticks to Princess of Streaked Clouds, and so be blessed with many sons.

For several hours she had watched her lord through her eyelashes, and she discerned that there *were* minor differences between the foreigners. Her lord was shorter than most, but he had a fine, loud voice, and he could spit better than any. He was a better spitter than even the pig-coolie of the big house.

She realised, with a jolt, that her lord was standing over her. Her first impulse was to kowtow, but she restrained herself, and merely bowed. Dando proffered a tin plate bearing the inevitable salt beef, boiled peas and biscuit. ''Ere,' he said. He was off-hand, self-conscious. ''Ere's yer vittles. It ain't cook-shop stuff, but it's no soddin' good complainin'.'

She took the plate with both hands. '*Hsieh*!' Being given food by a master was confusing, and she knew she must not eat while he watched, despite her hunger.

Dando cleared his throat. 'Wot's yer name?' She did not understand.

He pointed to himself. 'Me, bull chillo, Dando.' He paused. 'Dando.' Then he pointed at her. 'You, cow chillo —?'

She nodded shyly, comprehending. 'Yü. Cow chillo, Yü.'

Dando frowned. 'Sod it, I know yer' bleedin' you. I'm bleedin' me.'

Yü nodded again. 'Cow chillo, Yü.'

Dando shrugged. 'That's wot yer git fer askin',' he told himself. Then he considered. 'Orlright, yer' bleedin' You. It don't make no difference, see? You.' He took a pace backwards and eyed her critically as she stood, plate in hand, gaze lowered. 'There ain't much of yer, is there? I mean, yer don't exackly 'ave any *generous parts*, do yer?'

Yü did not have any generous parts. She was slight, slimbodied, with small breasts. Her feet, even if unbound, were still tiny, and her clasped hands were hardly larger than a child's. Studying her, however, Dando was aware that, when her bruises had disappeared, she would have a face of no mean beauty, delicately boned, her eyes brown and almond-shaped, her skin clear and flush-cheeked. Her hair, thickly black, lay in a neatly plaited coil over her shoulder.

'Still,' he conceded, 'yer ain't too bad.' He whistled softly through his teeth, contemplatively. 'I've seen a lot bleedin' worse.' She was not, he decided, bad at all. In fact — 'if yer 'ad a skirt instead o' them soddin' trousers, an' a 'at with a feather' — No, somehow he was unable to associate her with whale-bone stays and high-heeled, buttonsided boots, and piled hair would be incongruous. On the other hand, how could he walk a woman in nankeen trousers down the Borough Road?

But he wasn't going to, was he? When the time came he would give her a little cash and then cut his stick.

How did one marry a Chinese woman, anyway? Among the crowded slums of London's poor there were few formal marriages. A man and a woman decided to share a roof and a bed, and simply did so. Dando would have been surprised if told that his own father, Matt Dando, had been married to his mother, and his interest in such a fact academic and short-lived. A few ritualistic words from a clergyman did not create a union. Men and women did. Nor would such a ceremony prevent subsequent infidelity or desertion. A man's fist was a far more effective deterrent.

'Look 'ere,' Dando said. 'I've been thinkin', see? You wanchee belonga me, heya? Alla same one-piecey wife. You cook food, plenty, washee clo'es. Can? Dando werry number-one good-ah, see?'

Yü could not contend with the rapid flow of pidgin but, intuitively, she gleaned its intelligence. Her eyes fell, abashed. Then, unable to restrain herself for another moment, she fell to her knees and lowered her forehead to the road. 'Gawd strewth,' Dando grunted, 'yer don't 'ave ter keep doin' that, see? It ain't bleedin' proper.'

'*Wo ken hsien-sheng ch'u.*' I will follow you, Lord, she whispered. Yü, also, would never have considered herself of sufficient importance to justify a marriage ceremony. Only very special women were married, and even they sat apart in silence as the men celebrated. She had watched a marriage feast, with a table laden with roast duck and sucking pig, steamed crabs in ginger sauce, maiden-hair seaweed and bitter melon, with the men growing progressively drunker on twelve-year-old rice spirit in which powdered tiger-bones had been steeped — which fortified the nerves, rendered the childless prolific, and stimulated youth-like spirits in the old.

Even had she been a concubine with flower feet, she could not have envisaged marriage. The Master would choose her name from his list and she would lie at the foot of his bed, naked, awaiting the honour and utmost happiness that her lord had condescended to bestow upon her.

Yü remained with her face to the ground, ashamed that she was so worthless. Her lord deserved better — a hibiscus-scented, peach-breasted, willow-browed, jade-fleshed, mooncheeked maid, able to sing and perform the Dance of the Rainbow-coloured Sleeves. And she was only a menial with unbound feet.

'Fer Chris' sake, git orf the ground,' Dando grimaced. 'Ye're jumpin' up an' down like a monkey on a soddin' stick.' He waited until she rose, then nodded. 'Orlright, then, that's settled. Until further orders, ye're Missis Dando, see? Yer kin start fatigues tomorrer — boots an' belts spit-cleaned, collect tea from the "bobbers", an' 'ot water fer shavin'. I'll show yer 'ow ter use a cleanin' rod. Then there's rations. Yer kin give the beef a shock in the kettle, but none o' yer Chinee muck, see? Then there's mendin' an' dhobeyin'.' He paused, calculating. 'I ain't got no objection ter jobbin' fer the others, but the booze money's mine — an' there'll be no bleedin' jiggin' out o' line, fer *anybody*, see? If there's any jiggin', I'll do it.'

Yü admired the rise and fall of the whiskers under his ears, not understanding a word.

12

'Married?' Lieutenant Shaw was incredulous. 'Goddammit, Dando, you can't *marry* a Chinese!' He was not entirely sure *why* Dando could not marry a Chinese, except that it just wasn't done. 'Indulge in impudicity if you must, but you know the regulations, man. If you want to marry *anyone*, you need the Colonel's permission. But a Chinese —?'

'Ah, but I ain't bein' married proper, sir,' Dando explained. 'An' I don't need the Colonel's permission fer not bein' married proper, do I?' He expanded. 'It's like not bein' proper anythin' — not bein' proper promoted, not goin' on furlough, not bein' boozed. If I ain't proper, then I ain't — an' if I ain't, I don't need no permission.' It was perfectly clear. Even Holloran had understood it.

Shaw insisted. 'In any case, wives don't follow campaigns, Dando. If you aren't married proper — *properly*' — he winced — 'then you aren't married at all.' He paused again to consider, then snorted impatiently. 'Dammit, in that case you're just maintaining a woman — a paramour —
'

'No, she's a bleedin' Chinee —'

'— in the lines, and that's against regulations. It's good for fifty over a gun-wheel.'

Lieutenant Shaw had lost a considerable degree of his animosity towards the Indian yallers of his company — or, more accurately, had been forced to concede that they were his best soldiers and should, with advantage, be treated with reserve. No finer tutors could have been provided for the less experienced 'griffins' who had accompanied him from England. At every halt, it was the yallers' field kitchen that was first burning, their tents first raised or first struck. They were excellent foragers, and Shaw and his company had never gone hungry when the commissariat failed. He had learned to turn a deaf ear to indignant accusations that, whenever the 2nd Regiment's beef cart had been rifled, the 60th's camp-kettles were always miraculously steaming. Shaw, too, was aware of his own increased confidence when, on hazardous occasions, he had Sergeant Garvin and his incorrigible yallers in his vicinity. He had been damn' grateful for them, b'God, at Tang Ku. Still —

'There ain't nuthin' against it in QRs, sir,' Sergeant Garvin said. 'It don't mention a word about Chinee wives, whether they're proper or not. If yer arst me, sir —'

'I'm not asking anyone, Sergeant. Queen's Regulations don't mention Patagonians, Mongolians, or Congo pigmies. If the woman's not a wife, with permission to be taken on the strength, then she's just a damned camp-follower. The orders are that native hawkers are permitted in the lines during the hours of daylight, but not women of a certain type. They're prejudicial to good order and discipline. That being so, Sergeant, if any man is apprehended, consorting in a certain fashion with a loose woman, it'll mean a gun-wheel and fifty.'

*

The last bugle had been quiet for several hours, with the tent-lines hushed and in darkness. A few tendrils of mist groped like white fingers around the feet of the officers' ponies tethered by the guard-tent, from which gleamed a solitary oil lamp. Between the columns of the nearby temple, the bats circled and swooped, seeking night insects, and from the temple's tower a deep-voiced gong boomed at minute intervals, indicating that, within, a lone priest passed the dark hours intoning scriptures for the dead.

Dando, firmly swathed in his blanket, was awakened from sleep by a prodding boot. 'Wot the bleedin' —?'

Holloran, the midnight picquet, his face submerged in the upturned collar of his greatcoat, was framed by the tent opening. 'Faith,' he hissed, 'hevn't I brought ye' missis, me ol' Dando? The guard-sergeant's snorin' loik an auld hog, an' I've laced up Lieutenant Shaw's tint from the outside. He'll be wantin' a bloddy pole-axe ter get himself out in the mornin'.' Beside his considerable bulk was the diminutive figure of Yü.

Dando raised himself on an elbow. 'Christ, yer'll git me spread, Irish, wi' fifty o' the soddin' best —!'

'Faith, let no man kape ye asunder, as blessed St Patrick himself said in the Botanic Garrdens, straight after the Larst Supper, bedad —'

'Sod orf,' Dando retorted, but was aware that someone had wriggled into the cocoon of his blanket. 'Sod *orf*! I've changed me bleedin' mind, see?' He paused. 'An' keep yer 'ands orf me privates!'

Holloran shrugged. 'Et's not the foinest place fer starrtin' ye' loif ev married bliss, shure et's not — wid twelve other men snorin' an' gruntin', an' O'Toole's socks an' orl, but wid ye' swate little darlint, orl hot wid wantin' —'

'*Wo chin li ti pan,*' Yü murmured.

'Don't it bleedin' *make* yer!' Dando spat. 'Don't a bloke git any soddin' choice?'

'Did I iver tell ye, me ol' Dando, ev the toim thet Hugh McGinty thort he wuz marryin' Biddy O'Dell? Shure, an' whin he marched up ter the altar, wid the majesty ev a paycock in his foin new cord'roys — who d'ye suppose wuz waitin', an' lookin' loik the ol' cat that's dhrunk the craym — ?'

'I don't bleedin' care if it was Molly Malone and 'er soddin' cockles an' mussels —!'

'Bedad, et wuzn't Molly Malone —'

'*Tsen yang lei shih ni*?' enquired Yü.

'Shiny arse-'oles —'

'If yer stopped hollerin' an' got on wiv it,' Moss Rose's voice spoke from the gloom, 'we'd orl git some soddin' sleep.'

'That's right,' added Edwin Wilson. 'Jes' dig yer toes in, see? We'll orl look the other bleedin' way. But don't shake the soddin' pole.'

'Ef ye shake the pole,' Holloran explained, 'they kin tell whit ye're doin', me jewel.'

'D'yer *think,*' Dando enquired, 'that I ain't never done it before? Well, I bleedin' 'ave, see? But not in the middle o' Paddington Station. Don't yer want ter blow a soddin' whistle, so's I know when ter start?'

Holloran considered. 'Faith, ye don't want a whistle. Et'd waken the bloody guard-sergeant. Why don't I jes' say "Wan, two, thray —"?'

'Gawd strewth — it jes' ain't true —!'

'Why don't yer jes' *git on wiv it*?' Moss Rose suggested. 'I don't care if yer do shake the soddin' pole. I'll 'old me feet up, see —?'

'An' whin ye've finished,' Holloran continued, 'he kin put his fate down.'

'Yer'd think, wouldn't yer,' gritted Dando, 'that a man could enjoy 'is sublime moments without a lot o' ignorant sods shoutin' 'im on like a bleedin' prize-fighter? 'Ow d'yer think I kin raise any 'eat, wiv the soddin' midnight picquet standin' over me wi' a gun? An' me feet don't reach the pole. *An'* I ain't givin' no animated bleedin' exhibishun, see? Why don't yer bugger orf back to yer fourteen paces each side o' the bleedin' guard-tent?'

Holloran was aggrieved. 'Bedad, an' is thet gratitude, me ol' darlint? Whin ye're squazin' an' kissin' under the blanket, will ye be thinkin' o' Rifleman Holloran — bloddy marchin' an' stampin' in the cauld fog outside — who brought the little jewel ter yez?' He slung his rifle over a shoulder. 'Shure, et's always thim thet's nearest ter ye thet hunts the most.' He was about to depart, then hesitated. 'I wuz thinkin', me ol' Dando. D'ye remember me tellin' ye about Chinee wimmin — bein' different an' orl? Seein', bedad, that ye' missis hes got reglashun fate, wid ye be supposin' —?'

Dando drew a deep, frustrated breath. There was a long pause, and then Yü gasped, '*Hi yah!*' Dando grunted. 'No, it ain't different, see? It's *exackly* the soddin' same — 'cept it ain't 'ad any wear yet.' Another pause followed. 'An' now I'm raisin' 'eat, so I won't 'ave no time fer bleedin' *teeter-teet*. Yer'd better bugger orf.'

*

The manner of her being brought to her lord was perplexing, but so many things were perplexing. She had been startled by his exploration, but doubtless it was the foreigners' custom to be satisfied that the flowery paths of their women were virgin, and Yü had opened her thighs, her flesh melting at his touch. Her heart pounded with a wonderful fear, but it was as nothing to the piquant moment when her lord's jade stem was joined to her flowery path, to drop dew into a blooming peony, and Yü knew at last the substance of utmost happiness. For a long time, as Dando snored, she lay awake, staring at the darkness, then cautiously reached above the blanket to touch with her finger-tips the whiskers below her lord's ears.

13

The Chinese negotiators, led by Ts-ai, Prince of Yi, the Emperor's cousin, had again agreed. If the foreign soldiers would halt, then Lord Elgin and Baron Gros, with an escort of 1,000 each, could enter Peking, the Celestial City, and the Treaty of Tien-tsin would be ratified. The Anglo-French diplomatic corps was quietly jubilant. They had been right all the time, and the confounded, fire-eating military wrong. It was true that wars were too important to be left for soldiers to manage, and there was still a hope of being back in Europe by Christmas. There might even be a visit to Windsor, a title or two, or a broad ribbon for a frock-coated chest.

There were still, however, a few matters to be decided — one, the site of the main Allied camp during the period of the final negotiations, and when and under what circumstances Lord Elgin would meet the Emperor himself to deliver a letter from the Queen. The British taxpayer deserved a full pound of flesh in exchange for the expense of the China Expedition.

On 17 September the British negotiating party left Headquarters for T'ungchow to finalise these last points. The party, mounted, consisted of the consuls Parkes and Loch, Colonel Beauchamp Walker, Quartermaster General of Cavalry, Commissary Thompson, *The Times* correspondent, Bowlby, and an attaché named de Normann. They were escorted by six dragoons and twenty Sikhs under Lieutenant Anderson. All were blithely unaware that the tentative agreement they had so laboriously achieved with the Chinese was a time-wasting farce, and that they were about to prematurely spring a gigantic trap.

It was a bright, almost spring-like day, and they rode, chatting unconcernedly, through a landscape of high, breeze-blown millet. Occasionally someone would comment on the unusually busy activity of Chinese troops and artillery batteries — but it could be of no account. Prince Ts'ai himself, in T'ungchow, had confirmed the cessation of hostilities.

But, on their arrival in T'ungchow, Prince Ts'ai and his aides were clearly uneasy, their attitudes obstructive. Every minor item of the agenda was subjected to prolonged debate and argument, until it began to dawn on even the complacent Parkes that the meeting was nothing more than another delaying tactic on the part of the Chinese. When the discussions finished, having achieved little, it was dusk, and too late to return to the Allied lines.

At dawn the British party conferred together. It was agreed that Parkes, Loch, Walker and Thompson, with the six dragoons and three Sikhs, were to return immediately to the Allied lines, whilst the remainder would stay, to maintain a British presence in Tungchow until the Army's arrival. The Chinese must be reminded that, this time, the British meant business.

But within an hour, Parkes and his companions were aware that something was very wrong. The millet-fields and water-courses were teeming with Chinese infantry, forming battle-lines. Gingall batteries were in position, overlooking the proposed Allied camping site, with pyramids of roundshot ready, powder-baskets open, and fuses lit. Squadrons of Tartar cavalry waited in low ground, hidden by the high corn, and military mandarins were everywhere, shouting, exhorting.

The party's progress was not, for the moment, disputed. The Chinese soldiers eyed them with curiosity, seeming mildly surprised, but nothing more, at their presence. The British were in distant sight of the Allied camp-lines when they made their fatal mistake. They decided to split their force.

There was no doubt that something was wrong. The Chinese were clearly preparing for battle, and General Sir Hope Grant, unsuspecting, could find himself marching into a hornets' nest. Harry Smith Parkes, nominally in charge of the negotiating party and its escort, entertained a fleeting hope that there existed some misunderstanding, the result of poor communication between the Chinese military and civil authorities. Prince Ts'ai had firmly emphasised that hostilities had ceased, yet General San-Ko-Lin-Sin was preparing a vast ambush of the site agreed for the Allies' camp. Parkes decided to return to Prince Ts'ai to protest.

Meanwhile his colleague, Loch, was to make a dash for the British lines, accompanied by two of the Sikhs, to warn Grant of the situation. Finally, somewhat foolhardily, Colonel Walker, Commissary Thompson, and the remaining five dragoons would stay where they were among the Chinese positions, to observe and, hopefully, to later report.

Loch's ride was achieved without incident, but he was somewhat disappointed to find that the news he carried evoked little surprise. The British had already observed the Chinese activity ahead and to flank, and Sir Hope Grant had halted to redispose his own forces and to throw out skirmishers. In a few more minutes he would have ordered an advance, and the Chinese were going to learn the truth of one of their proverbs — about catching a tiger by the tail.

Grant, however, decided to delay his advance for two hours, to allow Mr Parkes time to reach Prince Ts'ai in T'ungchow. Parkes and his companions were likely to be safer in the company of a Prince of the Imperial house than in the hands of the *luh-ying*, whatever the day's events. Grant recalled the episode of San-Ko-Lin-Sin and Private Moyse. He was more annoyed with the behaviour of Colonel Walker, who should know better than to play hero in the Chinese lines, to little advantage. The scarlet coats and white topees of the dragoons were clearly visible over the high millet that separated the two armies, and if a general action opened, they could never hope to escape.

It was Mr Loch who initiated the final indiscretion. Stung by the indifference shown towards his exciting ride, he volunteered to return to T'ungchow, to rejoin Harry Parkes. It was an empty gesture, perhaps made from a mixture of chagrin and bravado, but Sir Hope Grant, with a dozen problems to contend with, agreed. Even more incredible, a Captain Brabazon, of the Royal Artillery, offered to accompany Loch, and the pair turned their horses towards the Chinese.

*

Colonel Walker, Commissary Thompson, and the five troopers of the 1st Dragoons were in a predicament becoming increasingly uncomfortable. Ill-drilled columns of Chinese troops were arriving with every minute, trotting into line, halting, and loading their matchlocks. Worse, they were becoming truculent towards the tiny British party in their midst, catcalling and spitting. A mandarin, wearing a red button on his hat, rode past with an escort of Tartars, and Walker recognised him. It was San-Ko-Lin-Sin. The mandarin eyed them inscrutably, snarled a few words at an aide, then moved on. Seconds later a Chinese infantryman snatched at Walker's sabre. He kicked the man away with a spurred boot, ordering his party to trot.

Ahead of them was a commotion, of shouts and flailing weapons. A dozen Chinese were hacking at a French officer who, shockingly mutilated, his uniform shredded, seemed to be already dead. How the officer had come into enemy hands Walker had no time to speculate. Another shouting Chinese sprang at him from his blind side and, this time, tore his sword from its scabbard. Walker wrenched it back by the blade, gashing his hand. Simultaneously, someone thrust at Thompson with a lance. Fortunately, the commissary's heavy belt turned the lance-head, and it merely furrowed his rib-cage. The next moment the Colonel shouted for his party to ride for their lives. They rowelled at their horses, their heads low, scattering their assailants and hell-bent for the distant Allied lines. A fusillade of wild musket shots followed them, shouts and screeches, but they were away — one trooper with a slashed thigh — and then they were among the tall, shoulder-high millet, with the British tents ahead of them and the advanced picquet of the 3rd Foot tramping forward to cover their approach. B'God, it was damn' good to see a line of stolid British redcoats, all beef, oaths and sweat, in line and as imperturbable as their own Kentish cliffs. The glorious ol' bastards! They reined in a welter of dust.

The General's compliments, sir. You are to present your report immediately.'

The Colonel grimaced. This would be worse than the Chinese.

*

Mr Loch and Lieutenant Brabazon reached T'ungchow and located Bowlby and de Normann — who were blithely buying souvenirs, unaware of any impending unpleasantness. Parkes soon joined them, having come from a frustrating and fruitless meeting with Prince Ts'ai. Without hesitation, they started on their return to the British lines with the remaining Sikhs, but the ten-mile journey could not have been achieved within the two-hour limit set by General Grant, who, they knew, would not jeopardise his army's movements for the sake of twenty men. They had covered only a short distance before they heard the ominous rumble of the British guns, and could see the mushrooming spouts of exploding shells between them and safety.

'That,' observed Mr Parkes, 'seems to have torn a hole in it, chaps', then added, doubtfully, 'I wonder if these Chinese fellows know about diplomatic immunity?'

The Chinese fellows did not. Within minutes they were surrounded by a gesticulating mob, and they might have been pulled from their horses but for the intervention of an officer who, primarily concerned with exercising a mediocre knowledge of English, insisted on escorting them to the rear, to the village of Chang-chia-wan, and General San-Ko-Lin-Sin.

On entering the village, Parkes and Loch were led before the General, leaving the remainder in the unsympathetic hands of the *luh-ying*. Bowlby and de Normann, Lieutenant Anderson, Trooper Phipps, and eighteen Sikh cavalrymen were never seen again alive. With their hands tied behind their backs, and kneeling, they were beheaded before evening of that same day.

General San-Ko-Lin-Sin was viciously angry. His infallible plan — to lure the barbarians into a pre-arranged camping site, to surround them with a nine-to-one superiority, then butcher them — had misfired. No, that wasn't right. The perfidious barbarians had fired first, and even now were driving back his finest regiments in chaos, the Sikhs and dragoons scything down the fleeing Chinese in scores. San was going to have difficulty in persuading anyone that this was a glorious victory. This time both the Emperor's cousin and a younger brother were in the army's company.

It was infamous, it was treachery, San roared through his interpreter, as Parkes and Loch stood before him. The barbarians had broken the truce. They had attacked the unsuspecting *luh-ying*, who had been innocently gathering supplies and water for the foreigners' camp. The dark-skinned slaves of the barbarians were even now approaching Chang-chia-wan, their swords red with the blood of brave Chinese. Was there no honour among the English?

Parkes was thrown to the ground, his face rubbed in the dust. Was there any reason, asked San, why the pair of them should not be killed immediately?

But the rumble of gunfire was approaching fast, and the single street of Chang-chia-wan streamed with dispirited Chinese troops, flying from the closely following dragoons, Sikhs, and French Spahis. San-Ko-Lin-Sin had no desire to be caught with two headless British diplomats, or to be caught at all. He ordered them to be taken to Prince Ts'ai.

Ts'ai, however, was one move ahead of the General. He, also, had no desire to be captured. There was too much to be explained. His quarters were deserted.

Parkes and Loch, bound, were bundled into a cart which, with its lack of springs and the haste with which its driver urged his horses over the rutted road, battered them cruelly. It was some small compensation to recall that this was the manner in which the American ambassador. Ward, had been compelled to travel to Peking during the previous year. In Peking, however, Parkes and Loch were chained, then thrown into separate cells among the city's common criminals.

If one shot was aimed at the walls of Peking by a barbarian gun, they were warned, both would be executed instantly.

14

When the Saxons under Alfred were fighting the Danes, there had stood a town on this site, on the northern edge of the North China Plain — in the centuries that followed named successively Yenking, Tatu, Peiping, and finally Peking. The great Kubla Khan, emperor of the Tartars, made it the capital of China, which it remained, save for one brief lapse, under the later Ming and Manchu dynasties.

Peking became not a single city, but several — adjacent, but rigidly segregated. The Tartar conquerors occupied the Inner City, enclosed by a broad, 50-foot wall, and denied to the inferior Chinese, who built their own settlement outside — the Outer City.

The most beautiful and exclusive part of the capital was the Imperial City of the Ming and Manchu emperors, and enclosed within it was yet again the Forbidden City, or the Summer Palace, used only by the royal families and their retinues, and unknown to foreigners except for a few Jesuit priests of the seventeenth century.

Confusingly, the Summer Palace was not a palace in the accepted sense. It was a vast parkland, within its own walls, occupying eighty square miles and embodying two hundred main buildings, many of magnificent proportions, pavilions and gardens. There were lakes crowned with marble bridges, stocked with golden carp, and floating with miniature warships. Peacocks and other exotic birds strutted on green lawns, among dwarf trees and blossoming shrubs, and herds of tiny deer grazed. There were great baroque halls of audience, soaring pagoda roofs of gold and turquoise glazed tiles, gilded trellis, and grottoes filled with colour. Doves cooed and dragonflies hummed, rainbow-hued, among bronze dragons and tinkling waterfalls.

The Summer Palace had its human population — mandarins of the highest rank, but ready in a moment to grovel on their knees before the Son of Heaven, Lord of Ten Thousand Years, Brother of the Sun and Moon. There were notaries and tutors, astrologers and doctors, soldiers, musicians, artists, priests, and servants and groundsmen of every possible category. And there were the concubines.

The concubines were numerous, exquisite in body, perfect of manners, and carefully guarded. Many were the daughters of high-ranking families, the gifts of favour-seekers. They came from every corner of China, from Siam, Malaya, Japan, Tibet, Manchuria, the chosen flowers of Eastern womanhood.

None had ever been European barbarians. There were European women available, in Hong Kong and Macao, not including acknowledged prostitutes, who might have eagerly sought favour in the Summer Palace, but barbarian women were repulsive, lacking any culture and the most elementary of graces. Their skin was coarse, and they did not even shave the hair from their bodies. They had disgustingly big feet, and the nauseating foods they ate tainted their breath.

But the eyes of an imperial concubine suggested the apricot, her eyebrows the crescent moon, and in those eyes the light was that of the silent waters of an autumn lake. Her teeth were white and tiny as the seeds of a pomegranate, her waist slender as a weeping willow, her fingers delicate as spring bamboo shoots as they plucked music from the strings of the chi'in. She smiled, her eyes lowered, but she never laughed, and she sat with her legs closely together. When the eunuch wrapped her, naked, in a great rug of sable or ermine, and carried her through the endless marble corridors of the palace to the innermost, guarded room, she lay passively, perfumed and lacquered, her hair jade-pinned, content in the supreme honour that was hers.

It did not appear remotely strange to a concubine — or, indeed, any female — that many women should be maintained for the pleasure of one man. A single pot served many cups with jasmine tea, but who had heard of one cup and many teapots?

The thousands of rooms of the numerous pavilions were rich with the treasures of many emperors — jades and porcelains beyond price, magnificent paintings, bronzes, enamels, clocks and statuettes. Furnishings of carved rosewood, ebony and ivory were upholstered in heavy silk of imperial yellow, embroidered with dragons in gold thread. Floors were spread with sable furs, sea-otter, ermine and silver fox, and chests and cabinets brimmed with bullion, jewels, watches and ornaments, many that had not been handled for centuries. One immense hall was piled with countless hundreds of rolls of silk, of all colours, but particularly of imperial yellow, the colour prescribed by law for the exclusive use of the Son of Heaven.

This, then, was the prize in the path of the advancing Allies — vast, rich, defenceless. Few British armies in history would have resisted its tempting glitter; to the less disciplined French it would be intoxicatingly irresistible. And it would be the French who reached the Summer Palace first.

15

Yü was not sure about the infants' urine. Several of the dishes she had prepared for her Lord and his companions had not been well received, and she had been ashamed. Two small boys had bartered their day's catch of freshwater shrimps and minnows for two gallons of coal oil that she had found inexplicably disowned by the guard-tent. She had carefully fried her acquisition, added the tender flesh of a puppy dog, lotus seeds and heart of cabbage, and garnished the dish generously with slugs and chicken feet. It had been fit for a mandarin, but her Lord's large companion had scrambled to his feet, bellowing. 'Turrds! Bloddy turrds! An' earwigs wid whiskers, be-dad! An' whit are thim unspaykable things?' He held up a chicken's foot. 'Did I iver tell ye, me oi' Dando, iv the toim Mrs O'Gorman found the big ol' toe en a loaf ev bread from McCormick's Bakery —?'

Nor had her Master been grateful when she had sewn the large symbol *Yüng*, for courage, on the back of his green tunic. No soldier should be without such a symbol, but the mandarin, whose name she knew was Shaw, had not been impressed.

It was Shaw, she decided, and to a lesser extent Sergeant Garvin, who exercised considerable influence over her Master's daily welfare. Shaw, then, should be the subject of a little bribery — squeeze. All officials, tax-collectors, magistrates, and particularly military mandarins, were susceptible to squeeze, and Lieutenant Shaw could be no different. Yü resolved to deal with Shaw first, and perhaps the Sergeant later.

Yü had no money, but she did have infants' urine. For days she had collected it in an old sherry bottle. But, of course, a menial could not openly offer squeeze to a mandarin. It must be extended subtly, unmentioned by either party in order that no face was lost. Yü carefully corked the bottle and, during a quiet moment, left it on the small camp table in Shaw's tent.

The officers of the four companies had had no mess wine for several days. The commissariat had foundered somewhere south of Chang Chia Wan, and native fermentations were a poor substitute. Shaw was puzzled when he found the full sherry bottle in his tent. Captain Williams of the Royals owed him a bottle of brandy, but the Royals were forty miles away. Still, dammit, a gift horse was not to be questioned, and Shaw, congratulating himself, took his prize to the mess.

'B'God. Sherry,' said Major Rigaud. 'That's damn' decent of you, Shaw.' Captain Warren and Lieutenants Merrah and de Vereker brightened expectantly.

'My pleasure, sir,' Shaw glowed. He filled five glasses.

'I always say,' offered Rigaud, 'that there's nothing quite like sherry, dammit. Ye can swill claret, or choke on port, but sherry —' He eyed his glass against the light. 'A delicate, golden hue, ye'll notice. The gentle child of sundrenched vineyards in the Jerez valley.' He paused, indulgently. 'Shaw, my dear fellow — since it's your sherry, perhaps you will offer the Loyal Toast?'

All rose to their feet, lifting their glasses. Shaw cleared his throat.

'Gentlemen. Her Majesty the Queen —!'

*

Sergeant Garvin stood unmoving as Lieutenant Shaw exploded. 'Goddammit, Sergeant! She's *got* to go, do you understand? First it's ducks' heads with blasted fish entrails, then stewed dog — and we didn't know till afterwards, when we found the head and fur. There's not a drop of coal oil for the lamps, and I shudder to think where the milk comes from — I've only seen pigs for weeks. But don't tell me, for God's sake. And now *this*!' He held up the half empty sherry bottle. 'The Major's still vomiting. God blast it! That woman's a confounded agent of San-Ko-Lin-Sin! She frightens me more than a brigade of Tartar cavalry! I wake up in the night, in a cold sweat, wondering what oriental horror I shall find on my breakfast plate —!'

'It's only the vittles, sir, that ain't much good. She's orlright wi' dhobeyin' an' sewin' —'

'Sewing? With Dando parading with a bloody great flag on his back, and a peacock's feather hanging from his shako?'

'It ain't exackly easy, sir.' Garvin rubbed his nose with a thumb. 'It's no good tellin' 'er ter sling 'er 'ook, 'corse she won't go. We can't reely march 'er orf at sword-point — an' anyway, when yer turns roun', she's back agin, bowin' an' shee-sheeing. Besides, she works like a buck nigger, an' the men 'ave a sort o' *regard* for 'er — and it ain't wot yer might think, sir. 'Cept fer Dando, only one man tried ter give 'er a touch-up, and 'ee near got 'is pills clawed orf. She's a sort o' *mascot*, yer see, sir, like the Taffs' goat, only goats don't darn socks an' dhoby shirts. An' she's gittin' better wi' the vittles. She's learnin'. Them four suckin' pigs we got fer two pairs o' of boots and a pound o' yaller soap — them weren't arf bad.'

The sucking pigs, Shaw conceded, weren't half bad, and the sauce had been succulent, even if unidentifiable. The Café Royal could not have provided better. Shaw heaved a breath.

'Goddammit, Garvin, just keep her out of my sight, that's all. One more decayed fish-head, one more chicken claw —' He left the threat unfinished. 'And if you breathe one word about this' — he lifted the sherry bottle — 'I'll have your stripes if it's my last act on earth. I have no desire to be written into the regimental records as the officer who presented the Loyal Toast in Chinese piss!'

*

All hope of an immediate peace had now disappeared, and the Allied armies pressed on towards Peking, outflanking an enemy garrison at T'ungchow. They had yet received no news of Parkes and his party. There was still spasmodic communication with the Chinese, and there was, in fact, a total of 37 prisoners, British, French or Indian, assumed to be in enemy hands, and the Allies were insisting that these be released before further negotiations were undertaken. In return, Prince Kung, the absent Emperor's younger brother, promised to free the prisoners as soon as the Allies withdrew, hinting that he could not be responsible for the hostages' safety if Peking was approached further. It was not a proposal that the Allies could seriously entertain, despite personal sympathies, and the advance continued.

The Chinese made their last determined stand at the village of Pa-li-ch'iao, barely ten miles from the Celestial City. In desperation they defended a bridge across a canal — the final obstacle — and it was here that the French Infantry made their greatest contribution of the campaign. With standards streaming and drums rolling, they charged, through a blizzard of shot, to take their bayonets to the Chinese batteries. A British observer might have remarked, wryly, that it was magnificent, but it was not war. Albeit, with the bridge forced, nothing now remained between the barbarians and the walls of Peking.

*

Yü sat on her haunches, cleaning one by one the yallers' rifles. Their spare boots already stood in a neat row, gleaming with black-ball. It having been pointed out to her that although a mixture of coarse sand and sesame oil, assiduously applied, could make dulled gunmetal glitter like silver, it did little for a rifle's performance, she now resigned herself to cleaning rod and rag. Sergeant Garvin had rescued Lieutenant Shaw's dress sword after it had been used to hack kindling, and returned it secretly to his valise. The point had been snapped off and the blade notched in several places, but fortunately the Lieutenant did not draw his dress sword very often. It was going to be interesting when he next did. Major Rigaud, to the end of his days, would never understand why the feet of his best pair of jackboots, of Russian leather, handmade by Hatchett, suddenly became white-painted. He did not know that all flowered-red-button mandarins should wear white-soled boots. Nor did the Major ever know that Yü had washed four hundred Enfield cartridges in hot soapy water, then laid them to dry in the sun, before being persuaded not to continue with the remaining Company ammunition.

'Yer can't expect everything at once, sod it,' Dando protested. "She's only been joined four weeks. 'Ow many recruits kin 'andle a rifle, build a field kitchen, forage for a company, an' cook vittles — after only four weeks?' He sniffed. "Whin I kin teach 'er ter shoulder arms, an' say, "Halt. 'Oo goes there?" instead o' "Stoppee now, what likee one piecee man?" — she kin stand bleedin' picquet.'

"The Divil! I'd niver hev thought ev ut!' admired Holloran. "Whin ye consider ut, bedad, there's no nayd fer a sodger ter get arf his arrse except ter draw his pay.'

"Them Frogs 'ave the right idea,' Dando went on. To concede that the undisciplined French had anything to offer the British required a major effort, but the *poilus* had retrieved a degree of respect by their recent, reckless assault on the bridge at Pa-li-ch'iao. "Did yer see them wimmin sodgers they landed in 'Ong Kong? An' the booze they carried in little barrels?' Several of the French units had been accompanied by their *cantinières* — seductive young mademoiselles, dressed in near-masculine, pantomime military attire, who sold brandy for a few sous to the troops during the day and more expensive favours to the officers after dark. 'It's a bleedin' good idea,' Dando said. 'Wimmin wi' barrels o' booze.'

'Or dogs,' Holloran nodded. 'Did ye know theer's dogs wid barrels o' booze? Orl ye does, bedad, is jes' lays down an' whistles.'

'After this,' Dando mused, 'things ain't never goin' ter be the same.' He eyed contentedly a dozen of the yallers' shirts, pegged to a clothes-line — then realised, with a jolt, that the detachment's last remaining Union Jack, which should have been fluttering over the guard-tent, was also hanging with the shirts. It was now a congealing confusion of red, blue and pink. Dando sighed.

'Since we left Chatham in 'fifty-one,' he hurried on, pretending not to notice, 'we've got a new barricks in Winchester. It's jes' our bleedin' luck, ain't it, ter git new barricks jes' when we're soddin' time-expired?' Fort Pitt, in Chatham, had been dirty, sordid and vermin-ridden, with men, women and children crowded into small, smoke-clogged barrack-rooms. There had been Corporal Garvin's wife, Meg — still in Calcutta — and Katie Lawrence, who had soaped his socks and drained his blisters with a needle. 'I wonder,' he frowned, 'wot 'appened ter Katie Lawrence?'

Holloran shrugged, then spat. 'Shure, she hed a hearrt ev gold, but she wuz no jewel ev a colleen ter turrn a man's hed wid bloddy admeerashun. And wid thray brats, bedad —?'

*

Katie Lawrence would have turned no man's head. She was a slovenly Irishwoman, coarse-mannered and hard-swearing, but with a loyalty to her man that was unshakeable and a dedication towards mothering the young recruits during their first weeks in an unfeeling Army. Both Dando and Holloran owed much to Katie Lawrence.

Chosen by lot, only five of the twelve wives in the Chatham barrack-rooms had been permitted to accompany the draft to India, and Katie had drawn the throat-choking scrap of paper marked 'Not to go'. They had last seen her standing motionless on a rain-swept Gravesend jetty, with three children clutching at her sodden skirts, as the troopship *Simoom* threshed into mid-river. She did not wave, and George Lawrence stood on the boat-deck, as if carved from stone, the wetness plastering his hair to his forehead, for a long hour after the tiny figures had disappeared into the rain haze astern. That had been nine years ago.

*

What did a homeless, penniless woman do when she had three brats, when she had no skills in needlework, shop-keeping or factory work, no physical qualities to attract a benevolent provider — even if she so desired? If she achieved a parish admittance order, there was the workhouse, which would separate her from her children. There was only one alternative, one to which thousands of women, faced with starvation, turned every year.

There were prostitutes of every social level, from the fashionable beauties with their own Knightsbridge houses and carriages, to the ravaged drabs who haunted dockside alleys, wheedling coppers from drunks and lascars in exchange for a few minutes against a wall. Between these extremes were the loiterers of Piccadilly and Covent Garden, the frilled night-house ladies, casino dancers, cigar-shop girls, the underpaid governess or lady's maid — and, worst of all, the child prostitutes of nine or ten who plucked at the sleeves of male passersby with shameless proposals.

Katie Lawrence was nothing if not practical. If she entertained any qualms about prostitution, she quickly thrust them aside. She had lost her man for the next ten or twelve years. Indeed, he might never return. In India there awaited cholera, smallpox, dysentery, malaria, pneumonia, and enemy bullets, and the odds on her becoming a widow were high. Besides, she had three small mouths to feed. Harriet was six, William three, and Beatrice two.

Katie was no longer young. She had no pink and white complexion, no mincing walk, no hourglass figure with breasts pushed high by tight-laced corsets, but she had a sharp wit, a repertoire of barrack-room songs and oaths, and she could hold her liquor better than most men. Katie was an ideal companion for soldiers, sailors and watermen who wanted several hours of carousing before tugging their women to a mattress, by which time they were often too stupefied to make more than a token effort to achieve a shilling-worth of carnal satisfaction, too fuddled to count their change, or distinguish a shilling from a sovereign. Katie knew men, and she and her little ones were not going to starve.

The first few days, in Gravesend and Tilbury, provided thin fare, and it rained incessantly, coldly. Even the cheapest of lodging-rooms could not be acquired by a shabby woman and three children without some payment in advance, and they sheltered under dockside timber, under carts, dodging the watchmen seeking out just such vagrants as these — but the rain was an ally as well as a discomfort. The watchmen, too, preferred shelter and a glowing brazier to patrolling a rain-soaked pier.

With a few shillings earned, however, there was food, and then the long tramp to Woolwich, where the Artillery depot and the Naval dockyard between them offered better prospects. Here, also, was the tiny tenement room, dirty and damp, but a roof — and Katie swore that she and her brood would never again be without a roof. Later there was a second room. As the children grew older, Katie could never, without embarrassment, submit to the panting lust of a stranger while they watched with puzzled eyes.

She was careful with her earnings, hoarding every ha'penny, but the children were fed, with clean, second-hand clothes, and shoes to their feet. The rent was regularly paid. Katie, too, kept herself washed and neat — no beauty still, but she caught the attention of men who desired better than the usual draggled, gin-soaked creatures who reeled from tavern to tavern, unscrupulous and unfeminine. Her regular patrons included an elderly tugboat captain, a troop sergeant from the depot, and a Greenwich grocer who came every Monday at midday. There were bad occasions, from which she emerged with a blackened eye or broken lips, with the children screaming, and a confrontation with the pimping protector of rival prostitutes could mean cracked ribs from a lashing boot. It was a vicious, unsympathetic world, but Katie had never known a different, and she held on grimly. Slowly, very slowly, her little store of shillings and pennies began to grow.

She never heard from George Lawrence. He had no address to which to write, and Katie was illiterate. In any case, what could she tell him? Could she explain that she was a dockside whore, that his children were fed and clothed from the shillings and florins of sweating, cursing seamen, soldiers and bargees? In 1857 she learned of the Sepoy Revolt in Bengal, and of the decimating casualties of the 60th Rifles. Deep within her, something that had continued to glow with a dull red turned suddenly to grey ashes.

It was now only the children that mattered, and first of all Harriet. She was now twelve, a bright, pretty, intelligent girl — and she *knew*. Even so, Katie had hoped that she would be a shirt-finisher. It was hard work, but decent. For twopence-halfpenny she had to sew collar and wristbands, six buttonholes, and four rows of stitching on the shirt-front — a lengthy labour for twelve-year-old fingers, often in the yellow glimmer of an oil lamp — but it was decent.

Harriet, Katie resolved, would never walk slum pavements, offering her body to leering, beer-stinking men for the price of a meal. Harriet's whiteness would never be fingered by dirty Greeks and Italians, or lascar seamen. And, before God, Harriet would never marry a soldier.

But Harriet — intelligent, observant little Harriet — was not content with a reward of twenty-five pence for seven full days of painstaking labour. Her mother could earn that sum in a single hour.

Katie had never suspected. When she left the tenement during mid-morning, Harriet's fair head was already lowered over her sewing at the window, the smaller children finishing a breakfast of bread-and-dripping and noisily planning an expedition to Woolwich Common, where the volunteers were drilling. It was Katie's day for Greenwich, a day of pavement tramping.

When she returned, it was dusk, but there was no lamp-glow from the window, and William and Beatrice sat on the steps, chilled and hungry. They had been back, they claimed, for hours and hours and hours, but there was no Harriet, and the door was locked. Was there anything to eat? Where was Harriet?

Katie was puzzled, and a little frightened. Harriet ran occasional small errands, but never, if the children were to be believed, for hours. And the back-streets of Woolwich after dark were uneasy places for a girl of twelve to be walking.

Even as Katie lit the lamp, uncertain, Harriet arrived, breathless, and peeling off her thin cloak. She did not meet her mother's enquiring eyes, and her shoes were dusty, precisely as Katie's.

There was a knot in Katie's throat, but of course it could not be. There were hundreds of explanations. 'Shure, ye're late out, Harriet,' she admonished. 'Hev ye sewn ye' pieces?'

Harriet's eyes rose at last. They were tired, old. 'There's easier ways, ain't there?' she whispered. 'Like your'n.' She extended an open palm, in which lay two florins.

*

The British advance guard and flanking parties had reached Yuan Ming Yuan, north-west of Peking, and before them lay the walls of the Imperial Summer Palace. The troops had marched all day, with considerable numbers of enemy infantry falling back before them, but always out of reach. It had been tiring and frustrating. Somewhere on the left flank were the French, but nothing had been seen of them, either, even by searching cavalry patrols. Now the British had reached the agreed rendezvous, and there was still no sign of the French — nothing but a Tartar cavalry picquet withdrawing through the Tih-shing Gate as the Sikhs approached.

Where the hell were the damn' French? The arrangements had been clear enough — a steady advance, British to the right, French to the left, converging on Tih-shing. It could hardly be simpler for de Montauban, and there was little in his path except a few uncoordinated groups of fleeing *luh-ying*. Thirty thousand Frenchmen couldn't vanish into thin air, even in China. The handful of French liaison officers with Sir Hope Grant's staff could offer no excuses.

Grant was annoyed at de Montauban's failure to acquaint him with any new development that may have arisen, and the British now apparently had a nakedly exposed left flank. Not that this, under the circumstances, posed any great problem. The bulk of enemy forces had retreated northward of Peking, a disorganised rabble, and the Emperor, Grant had learned, was at Ge-hol, a hundred miles from the city, with his thirteen wives and younger children. Only three hundred eunuchs had been left to defend the Summer Palace. Still, the unexplained absence of de Montauban, who had always insisted on protocol, was a discourtesy, to say the least. Grant did not intend to retaliate. The Allies had agreed that they would enter the Forbidden City together, and here it was for the taking. However, it could wait for another day. Grant ordered the British forces to bivouac among the scattered houses of Yuan Ming Yuan.

*

De Montauban insisted later that it had been entirely the fault of the British, who in their advance had veered to their left, completely across the path of the French on their flank. This seemed hardly credible, nor did the General explain why he had not immediately sent gallopers to the British to draw attention to the error, if it had occurred. Furthermore, the British had arrived punctually at the agreed rendezvous, Yuan Ming

Yuan, whereas the French had disappeared from the left flank, swinging behind the marching British to the extreme right, to find themselves, oddly, not at Yuan Ming Yuan, but at the Se-che Gate, a considerable distance in the opposite direction to that in which the British patrols had been seeking them all day. It was all very strange and, in view of the events that followed, not altogether surprising that there would be British mutterings of foul play.

To a degree, British suspicions were justified. De Montauban had always resented being considered a junior partner to Grant, although the latter had done everything possible short of jeopardising military operations to ensure parity of national reputations. Despite the far smaller number of French, the leadership of the column had been taken in turns, daily, and an attempt had been made to involve French troops in every set-piece action. Even so, there was much that the French could not do. Their cavalry consisted only of a few Moroccan Spahis, they were short of horses, mules, carts, and they had only light, mountain-type artillery. The British, largely because of the availability of troops in India, the vicinity of a base in Hong Kong, and a massive fleet, were superior in every department. They did not need the French, and it was inevitable that they should consider their Allies' contribution merely a token, political one.

It could hardly be suggested that de Montauban had anticipated all the events that followed his change of route, but it is certain that he had contrived to march the Tricolour into the Summer Palace before the Union Jack. He could make his excuses afterwards, when it was too late, and his promotion to Marshal of France was well worth a little unpleasantness from Grant. What de Montauban did not know, however, was that the vision of the helpless Summer Palace would turn his army into an undisciplined, uncontrollable, loot-crazed mob. British officers attached to de Montauban's staff established contact with Sir Hope Grant at dawn, and Grant, accompanied by a troop of dragoons, several aides and correspondents, rode for the French camp. When they arrived, they were faced with a scene of utter chaos.

*

Maddened by loot-hunger, the red-trousered French infantry burst under the Se-che Gate, a tidal wave through a burst dam, flooding across the lawns and smashing down shrubs and flowerbeds. Protesting officers were flung aside, helpless — and, aware of their helplessness, shrugged, then ran for the distant, defenceless pavilions, where the accumulated treasures of a thousand years waited, where any man could take as much as he wished, as much as he could carry. Carved and gilded doors of priceless workmanship were splintered with boots and rifle-butts. Blaspheming men tore down tapestries, then threw them underfoot to grasp a jade or an ivory. Exquisite porcelain shattered, and delicate jewellery was torn between disputing fists. The concubines scattered, screeching, their lacquered hair ravelled, but nobody wanted concubines, only loot. Men staggered under impossible loads of incongruous values — bolts of silk, furs, chinaware, kitchen utensils, stuffed animals, carpets, clothing, furniture, statuettes and antique weapons.

The two eunuch gate-keepers had been killed within seconds, and several others were sprawled among broken debris, bayoneted or shot. Peacocks fluttered crazily among steel-shod feet, and men scrabbled on their knees, thrusting their arms into chests of coin and trinkets. Ancient parchments by the hundred, the writings of centuries, littered paths and floors, trodden and spurned, and the herd of tiny deer streamed, terrified, across the park, seeking the trees. A thousand white pigeons exploded into the sky. The red and blue tidal wave swarmed on, engulfing and destroying, teeming into the Hall of Majestic Peace, the Palace of Earthly Tranquillity, the Pavilion of Blending of Earth and Heaven, the Hall of Precious Harmony.

*

'It'd make a bleedin' good beer garden,' Dando opined. 'Yer cud git 'undreds in 'ere. If I was in charge' — he pointed at the Temple of Heaven — 'I'd put seats orl 'round, see? Wi' gas lamps. Then Katie 'Amilton's young wimmin servin' the booze an' flauntin' their parts — but not too bleedin' brazen. That frightens orf the respectables. Yer wants a good name, wi' a bit o' foreign mystery — like Casino de Venus — an' a German band. There's got ter be bang-up entertainment, one night a prize fight, the next night a rat-killing contest, an' so on. Parrots an' monkeys — an' niggers. The wimmin likes ter see niggers. They makes 'em shiver, see — or an Indian chief walkin' on 'ot coal wiv 'is bare feet —'

'Shure, en Phaynix Park —' Holloran said.

'Bitter beer an' gin,' Dando insisted. 'Yer kin sell cheap champagne an' moselle ter the toffs fer twelve shillin's a bleedin' bottle, an' Stinko cigars like they was Corona Supremos. They only reads the label, see? Give 'em a bit o' *distrackshun*, like a judy skewin' 'er buttons, orl accidental, or a bit o' the ol' finger, an' they'll drink bleedin' coach-varnish.'

'Et's the truth,' Holloran agreed sadly. 'Et's loik the potheen ut Smyley's, bedad. The first bottle es brewed by the saints thimselves, by the magic hands ev Medb ev Connacht en person. Then, whin ye're ridin' on the wings ev angels, shure, Smyley brings out the stuff thet wuz boiled en the pig-tub, an' theer's no bloddy sense in ye. It's the next bloddy mornin', faith, whin ye' brain turrns ter hot glue, wid broken glass behind ye' eyes, an' a mouth loik Bengal rot —'

'*Samshu* pidgin plenty welly bad,' Yü interceded, 'alla same too many piecee bleedin' devils —' She had lost much of her apprehension towards the soldiers. 'Muchee soddin' bad joss, heya?'

'Nobody arst yer, ye slant-eyed whore,' Dando retorted, but not unkindly. 'An' not so much o' the bleedin' cussin', see? This ain't the soddin' Navy.'

'*Yu shih mo mao ping*?' Yü pouted.

'Don't it *make* yer?' Dando spat. 'If she don't cuss yer in English, she calls yer a bleedin' pub-crawlin' lush in Chinee.' He was, in fact, rather proud of Yü's education. With no lack of encouragement from the yallers, she had developed a range of barrack-room oaths that would not have shamed her in Portsmouth or Aldershot. When they got home, Dando mused, it was going to be bleedin' funny —

But, of course, Yü wasn't going to Portsmouth or Aldershot. Or anywhere.

*

Sir Hope Grant and the British were incensed. Vainly did the embarrassed de Montauban roar orders at his officers to halt the savage plunder of the Summer Palace. Nothing could have curbed the madness that gripped the French as, in their thousands, they roamed the palaces and pavilions, contemptuously deaf to all pleas for restraint. What they could not carry they destroyed. Great mirrors were shattered, chandeliers shot at, lacquered panelling smashed, and the private rooms of the Emperor himself wrecked beyond recognition. Of the British, only a few

Sikhs and dragoons, and a handful of fortunate officers, managed to enter the Summer Palace before most of the more easily transportable spoil had gone. From surrounding villages, Chinese peasants swarmed to join the French, only to find themselves forcibly deprived of their own prizes and compelled into service as porters by the invaders. Every means of conveyance was seized, and the French, who had reached the Palace with scarcely a wheeled vehicle, departed with three hundred loaded wagons.

*

Yü had been missing since Reveille. 'Where the soddin' 'ell is she?' Dando sulked. There had been no hot water for shaving, no early tea, no polished boots, and a disgruntled Lieutenant Shaw had emerged from his tent after a breakfast of half-cooked porridge stirabout that would have been accepted, unquestioned, three months ago. Shaw had become discriminating.

Beyond the Se-Che Gate there was a suggestion of smoke above the pavilion rooftops, and several times they had thought they had heard distant shots, but the orders had been to stand firm, There were no familiar throngs of ragged hawkers, jostling to sell eggs and fruit, and they had watched scores of furtive Chinese streaming through the gate into the sacred parkland of the Summer Palace. They had seen the like before, in Meerut and Delhi, of hungry, loot-seeking peasants emboldened by the absence of authority and their own numbers, treading where they had never dared before. Yü, also, had disappeared, and at noon she was still absent.

'When she does bleedin' muster,' Dando promised, 'she'll 'ave a sore arse from my belt-buckle. She won't soddin' do it agin, I kin tell yer.' But perhaps she wouldn't muster. 'That's bleedin' gratitude, see? That's what yer git.' Perhaps he had seen the last of Yü.

'Wimmin's quare, so they are,' nodded Holloran. He had resigned himself to cleaning his own rifle. 'Shure, an' I'm thinkin' ut wuz luck I had wid them six wimmin in the ship.'

'The luck of a bleedin' pox-doctor's clerk,' Dando affirmed. It wasn't the salt beef and biscuit, sod it, and he was capable of cleaning his own soddin' bundoo. He was reluctant to concede it, but it was something else, and if he had been asked to define it, he would have choked. 'Jes' wait,' he vowed, 'till she musters. I ain't 'aving it, see?'

At two in the afternoon the Dragoons' bugler was sounding off 'Boots and Saddle'. General Sir Hope Grant, it was rumoured, had returned from the French camp, white faced and dangerously angry, and it was an ill-chosen moment for the provost to report the arrest of a coolie for the petty crime of stealing a pair of boots. The General ordered the man to be flogged immediately, then sent his aides galloping with instructions for the cavalry to be mounted. The infantry would follow as quickly as tents could be struck.

'Move yer arses,' Garvin shouted. 'Field order an' sixty. No packs, tents or blankets — they'll foller by wagon.' Major Rigaud was briefing his juniors. 'Best greens and dress swords,' he ordered. 'We're making a ceremonial entrance.' Garvin flinched. 'Christ,' he whispered.

Dando laced the boots that had not seen black-ball that morning, then paused. 'Irish,' he said slowly, 'I ain't bleedin' goin'.'

Holloran, with the untrammelled perception of simple people, carefully unwrapped a fresh tobacco plug, eyed it thoughtfully, then bit expertly. 'Shure, an' didn't I know it, me ol' darlint?'

'When yer go,' Dando went on, 'I'm goin' ter be missin'.'

'When *thay* go, me jewel,' corrected Holloran, 'bedad, there's goin' ter be two blank files.'

'Sod orf. It's my bleedin' woman, ain't it? *My* bleedin' woman. D'yer know what 'appens ter deserters in the face o' the soddin' enemy?'

Edwin Wilson placed down the tin plate that carried his hard-tack, then spat. '*Three* blank files.'

'*Piss* orf!' Dando ejaculated. '*Piss orf*!'

'I told yer once,' Garvin said. 'Git fell in.'

Moss Rose sighed. 'There's a tide in the affairs o' every bleedin' man,' he quoted, 'when yer take it at the flood, leads to a soddin' penal battalion.' He sniffed. 'I ain't goin', neither.'

'Funny,' Jim Bathurst decided, 'yer took the words out o' me mouth.' He took off his shako, placed it on the ground, then stamped on it.

There was a long silence, then the faint shout of a distant troop sergeant. 'B Troop —! Prepare to mount —!'

Garvin's measured growl was scarcely louder. 'I don't often give orders twice, and I ain't never done three times. Yer ain't recruits. Yer all near time-expired men, an' yer've been read the Articles o' War.' He paused. ‘All right, then. Likely I didn’t say it plain, an’ likely nobody ’eard — so I’ll say it jest agin.’ He paused once more. ‘Git fell in.’

Nobody moved.

‘There’s bleedin’ devotion for yer,’ Dando grated. ‘If yer’d orl kept yer soddin’ mouths shut, I’d ’ave been orf, easy. But yer’ve got ter play the thin red line o’ bleedin’ ’eeroes, ain’t yer?’ He snorted. ‘Yer kin git shot, see? Or five years o’ black gang, breaking stones on the soddin’ roads.’ Sepoys in India had been sentenced to eight years of penal servitude for simply refusing to accept suspect cartridges, and that had been in peacetime. ‘And yer think that’s worth one slant-eyed little bitch of a bleedin’ Chinee woman — ?’

Sergeant Garvin drew a deep breath. ‘Dando — yer know yer can’t take ’er with yer. Yer’ve always known it. Nex’ week, or nex’ month — sometime — she’s got ter be told ter bugger orf. If she’s already slung ’er ’ook, she’s saved yer the trouble, see?’ He turned to scowl at Dando’s companions. ‘An’ none of yer’s goin’ ter fartin’ change anythin’ by defyin’ orders. I ain’t a man fer goin’ belly-achin’ ter soddin’ officers, an’ it’s lucky fer yer that my ear-’oles are bunged up, see? I ain’t ’earing proper today, an’ I ain’t ’eard a bleedin’ word yer’ve said — but if yer ain’t all fell in, shouldered an’ facin’ front, in ten seconds —’

‘Yer ain’t got it right, Sar’nt — nor ain’t them.’ Dando was subdued. ‘I know the little whore ’as got ter go — some time. Likely she ’as ’ooked it, but maybe she ain’t, see? Suppose she was foragin’. Jes’ suppose. There’s a thousand ragged-arse Chinamen over there who’d as soon kick a woman ter death as spit. Worse, there’s the bleedin’ Frogs. It’s been nine bleedin’ hours, an’ she ain’t been nine soddin’ hours before.’ He hesitated. ‘It ain’t that she’s got ter go, see? It’s jes’ that when she *does go* —’ He halted again, baffled and angry. ‘SOD IT! A man’s entitled ter *feelin’s*, ain’t ’ee? Suppose she *is* a slant-eyed bleedin’ Chinee? Suppose she *is*! I wudn’t change ’er, see? I wudn’t change ’er fer a titled tart wi’ whalebones an’ a carriage, an’ a thousand poun’s in the bleedin’ bank!’ He glared belligerently. ‘An’ if anyone wants ter say anythin’ —?’

Nobody had the slightest desire to say anything, but Major Rigaud was strolling towards the men grouped around Garvin. ‘What’s the delay, Sergeant —?’

Garvin turned reluctantly, his honest, ruddy face twisted with uncertainty. At that moment, however, there was a heaven-sent diversion. Lieutenant Shaw howled. In his hand he held aloft his dress sword, the blade of which was an eight-inch stump of mangled steel. He had flung the scabbard to the ground, then followed it with his shako. 'God in Heaven!' he roared. 'Look at it! *Look* at it! Goddammit — is there no *end* to it?' He raised his eyes. 'Is there no *pity* in those clouds? Forty pounds from Wilkinson — forty blasted pounds!' He closed his eyes.

'Christ,' breathed Garvin.

'Shure, et's a bent ol' sword, so 'tis,' Holloran observed. 'Bedad, I've niver seen sich a bent ol' sword. Ef I hed a sword loik thet, faith, I wudn't hev it.'

'Hi yah! *Hsien sheng kan shih mo shih*?' enquired Yü. She had suddenly appeared from nowhere, completely unconcerned, clutching against her hip a pannier from which dangled the lifeless necks of several ducks, bouncing elastically as she walked. 'Soddin' ducks welly high plice, no bleedin' eggs. Too muchee *Flogs*, bam-bam, alla same.' She gazed at the men innocently, and the men stared at her. Lieutenant Shaw choked, and Major Rigaud savagely ground a half-smoked cheroot into the earth with the heel of a white-soled jackboot. '*Dammit* — is *that* who we're waiting for?' He whirled on Shaw. 'Lieutenant —! Have you forgotten we're supposed to be fighting a bloody war? Get those men marching! And for God's sake — what's *that*?' He pointed to the broken sword in Shaw's hand. 'Another of your blasted, stupid jokes? When do you intend to *grow up*?'

*

The British share had been negligible, but there were a few worthwhile finds. Several staff officers had stripped the trimming from a cottage roof, spurned by the French as only brass, but which was subsequently found to be gold, worth £9,000. Two officers of the 60th purchased cheaply a set of handsome enamels, destined to become regimental mess property, and General Grant insisted that de Montauban shared a roomful of gold ingots that had not disappeared into the French camp.

And the French camp, for days, assumed the appearance of a vast, exotic market, offering, for exchange or purchase, silks, gold watches, strings of jewels, jades and furs, costumes and court robes, silver, bronzes and tapestries. It was here that the British, particularly the officers, achieved a degree of satisfying revenge, for the French soldiers had little idea of the true value of their booty, and would cheerfully sell a bolt of magnificent silk for a dollar note — worth 4/6d — or a bottle of rice wine. Even so, many of the French accumulated tolerable fortunes, remaining drunken, disorderly and unmanageable for a week.

From the public auction of material achieved by the British, which realised £8,000, supplemented by specie amounting to £18,000 surrendered by the French, every private soldier in Grant's army received £4 in prize payment.

*

On 8 October the two British consuls, Parkes and Loch, with five Frenchmen and one Sikh, were returned to the Allied lines in carts. A few days later they were followed by three more French and ten Sikhs, all terribly emaciated, with one dying the same evening. No further prisoners were returned alive, and the survivors told how they had been kept bound for weeks and repeatedly threatened with death by their gaolers, whose malevolence, particularly towards the Sikhs, increased progressively as the Allied armies neared Peking. If the captives appealed for food or drink, they were punched, kicked, or stamped upon. Dirt was crammed into their mouths, and the cords that bound their wrists were repeatedly soaked with water, so that they shrank, biting into the flesh and draining the hands of circulation. From the gangrene that followed, four Sikhs had died in agony while the Chinese jeered.

Then, on the 17th, cavalry vedettes at the west wall sighted an approaching caravan of Chinese carts, escorted by twenty Tartars. As the dragoons jingled forward, the Tartars scattered. The carts carried rough coffins, each containing a decapitated body, so decomposed as to be unrecognisable except by its tattered clothing. They were the remains of the attaché, de Normann, Lieutenant Anderson, Trooper John Phipps of the King's Dragoon Guards, Mr Bowlby of *The Times*, and eight Sikhs of Fane's Horse. Only Captain Brabazon, of the Royal Artillery, and the Frenchman, Abbe de Luc, were unaccounted for, and remained so, for ever.

16

'It was the bleedin' 'oomidity larst time,' Dando told Holloran, 'but *larst* time we didn't 'ave sheepskin coats, an' fur 'ats wiv soddin' ear'ole flaps.' The thermometer at Taku stood at 109 degrees. 'It's bleedin' diabolical, ain't it? We land 'ere in summer frocks, an' git soaked ter the marrer. Then, when it's 'ot enough ter put a 'undred and seventy men on the sick list, we're orl dressed up like bleedin' comic Eskimos!'

For four winter months the 60th Rifles had been in Tien-tsin, with all communications with the outside world severed. The Pei-ho had been solidly frozen for a hundred miles from its mouth, and reinforcements had been unable to land at Taku, returning to Hong Kong. The gunboats of the Royal Navy had been thatched over. There had been skating, amateur theatricals, and hunting expeditions. Despite the intense cold, health had remained excellent. Only now, with the battalion in Taku to embark for England, did the heat take its toll. Ninety-four men would never reach their troopship.

The ships lay at anchor in the hot Gulf of Pechihli — the *Anglo-Saxon*, *Walmer Castle*, the hospital supply ship *Winifred*, the horse transport *Calvados*, and the iron trooper *Simoom* —

'The bloddy *Simoom*!' Holloran grated. 'The bloddy, rot-guttin' *Simoom*! Ef there wuz anythin' spawned en the inferno ev Scáthach, et wuz the bloddy *Simoom*!' They knew the *Simoom*. For almost five months they had sweated and cursed, crammed into her maindeck, for the voyage from Gravesend to Bombay, ten years before. Five people, including two children, had died, thirty-three men had been flogged.

No soldier was able to regard an impending troopship voyage without flinching. The heat, stench, and confinement were not to be preferred to a campaign ashore. Troopships carried sufficient fresh water to allow every man a gallon per day, for twenty weeks — this for washing as well as drinking. During the weeks of equatorial heat, few men would waste precious fresh water on washing; they used brine, of which there was an endless supply, but which dried, itched and cracked the skin. There was a compensation. Every NCO and man received a daily free issue of a gill of rum. Officers had to pay for their alcohol. That, at least, was satisfying. The rum-drinkers, however, awaited with apprehension the 14th day of the voyage, after which they would be compulsorily dosed with a daily measure of lime or lemon juice, to fend off scurvy.

Rations comprised either beef or mutton, heavily salted, with vegetables — potatoes or onions, while they lasted — and oatmeal. There was always oatmeal. It filled an empty belly, albeit temporarily, and could be stored, rat-fouled, rank and dust-tasting, for years. Most ships also carried a deck-cargo of livestock, to be progressively slaughtered during the voyage — sheep, goats, ducks and fowls.

The *Simoom*, of 2,042 tons, had been laid down some years earlier, with her sister ship, *Megaera*, intended as the Navy's first iron frigates. Gunnery trials with an older iron vessel, however, had proved shockingly disappointing, and the Admiralty ordered that the two ships under construction should be completed as non-combatant troopships. Later, the reported results of the gunnery trials were found to be utterly misleading, but it was too late. The Navy would retain its wooden walls for many more years.

Now the *Simoom* lay in the bay, off Taku, a low black hull overlaid by an uninterrupted white band, and her long, rearing bowsprit rising and falling sluggishly. A weak trickle of smoke rose from a single, black funnel, over an upper deck cluttered with livestock pens, bales of hay, crates and baggage. She was a 'lobster pot' — a term of disdain applied to troopers by the Navy, which considered the troopship service an insalubrious backwater into which offending or less efficient officers were deposited and forgotten. As a result, troopship officers often tended to be of a disgruntled breed, unsympathetic towards their military charges — who were held wholly responsible for the existence of a service that blighted so many careers. Wherever the damn' Army travelled, the Naval officer cursed, it went on the Navy's back — and sometimes it rode blasted heavy.

'Jasus, Mary an' Joseph!' Holloran persisted. 'Wid ye belayve ut? Es ut murtherin' convicts fer Botany Bay we are? Or Quane's sodgers thet's been spillin' our blodd fer the Flag?' Nine hundred men of the 60th Rifles stood easy on the foreshore, their packs heaped and rifles piled, as they waited their turn to board the native sampans that would ferry them to the ship. A dozen hawkers shouted and wheedled to achieve last-minute sales of souvenirs, fruit, ice and juices, knowing that the foreign soldiers would be wishing to be rid of their last copper cash before it became useless.

'It ain't nuthin' yer've *done*, see?' Dando was attempting to explain to Yü. 'Chow plenty welly good.' It was, he knew, something he should have done before leaving Tien-tsin or, at least, in Sinho yesterday, but he had lacked the courage. Now — it had to be now. 'No can come my, heya? Sodgers can, cow chillo no can, savvy?'

Yü looked at him, refusing to comprehend. 'Can. Never mind.' Trailing from her hands were his rolled blanket, belt and cartridge wallet. She retreated a pace. 'Can!' she said, defiantly, but her voice broke. 'Bleedin' can!'

He shook his head, dumbly, his belly sick, yet angry with himself. He was a soft bastard, and no mistake. He was thinking of Chatham, ten years ago, when he'd seen Katie Lawrence emerge from the pay-sergeant's office, with a grey face and the scrap of paper in her hand — and George Lawrence, a speechless, whipped animal.

'No can,' he repeated. 'No wanchee. Finish.' He wasn't a soft bastard. Just a bastard. 'No wanchee one piecee woman ship my. No likee.' He pulled several crumpled dollar bills from a pocket, each of which would feed a coolie for a month. 'Cash you, buy 'em plenty, longa time.'

He held out the notes, but she did not glance down.

'*Tsên yang fei shih ni*?' Her voice was choked. She shook her head.

'It ain't no good arguing the bleedin' toss, see? Yer' time-expired. First turn o' the screws, orl debts paid. Yer ain't never been proper, an' I didn't soddin' *arst* yer, did I? Yer ain't on the *strength*, see? D'yer see that bleedin' floatin' coffin — ?' He pointed to the distant *Simoom*. 'It's goin' ter be stuff-gutted wi' sweatin', stinkin' men fer four months —' He was making excuses, and he knew it. Sod the Army. Sod China. Sod every festerin', rot-gutting, shitfaced bastard who made rules, an' laws, an' QRs —

Yü dropped to her knees. 'Chow plenty welly bad.' She put her forehead to the dust. 'Wo *chin li ti pan*. Worthless slave wanchee come alonga you, alla same. No can belonga Chinee. Bleedin' Dando missis.'

Only yards away, four or five Indian 'yallers' were gazing at the mud, whistling through their teeth and pretending indifference.

'It weren't my soddin' idea in the first place!' Dando directed the disclaimer towards his companions. 'Marry 'er, yer sez! But not proper, o' course, yer sez — then pat 'er on the 'ead and 'ook it! It was bleedin' simple, till yer gets ter the larst part, then it's 'ilarious —'

'Shure,' Holloran agreed sombrely, 'ut tears et ye hearrtstrings loik a drunken fiddler. Did I iver tell ye, me ol' Dando, ev the toim thet Rory Finnegan tuk his flute ter Donegal Horse Fair —?'

'At times like this,' suggested Moss Rose, 'there ain't nuthin' like a fistful o' rhino ter console a broken 'eart, We kin pass the 'at round. A dollar each, say?'

'No wanchee cash,' Yü sobbed from the ground. 'Useless cow chillo wanchee come you, alla same bleedin' sampan. No wanchee cash. Me no savvy cow chillo no come you —'

Several native boats had grounded in the filth-encrusted shallows, and Garvin was shouting for No. 4 Company to retrieve their rifles and packs. Dando sighed. 'It jes' ain't *on*, see? It always 'ad ter 'appen. Even if yer *cud* come, yer'd be 'opeless in England. Arsk anyone. It ain't no place fer Chinee wimmin.' He pushed the dollar bills into her loose fingers, then picked up his belt and cartridge wallet. Yü clenched her eyes. '*I lu p'ing an,*' she whispered.

*

When all the soldiers had crowded into the sampans and departed from the foreshore — all, that was, except for the ninety-four buried above the Taku high-water mark — Yü sat for a long time. Her predicament had not been entirely unexpected; she had suspected its coming for weeks, but had refused to contemplate it. If she erased the possibility from her thoughts, perhaps it would never materialise. But her Lord had gone to the big iron ship that smoked, evidently intending not to return, and she had been unable to tell him that her desire to accompany him was not merely the whim of a worthless woman-slave. He did not know that her belly was swelling under her nankeen smock, that she carried within her a man-child, almost four months old.

Yü knew it must be a man-child. She had offered many joss-sticks to Princess of Streaked Clouds, pleading that it should be so. He would be a fine child, fat like a puppy dog. He would have satin boots, white-soled like a mandarin's, and a small round hat with a red tassel. Yü had dreamed, stupidly, of taking her fine man-child to the house of P'u Sung

Ling, to proudly display to old Tien Mu the son of a foreign Lord, to bask in the awed respect of the kitchen menials who had beaten and pinched her, and of the barren concubines who — as her Lord said — were only bleedin' jiggin' machines. Was not Yü the first wife of a foreign Lord? Had she not seen mandarins of the Celestial City kowtowing to her Master? But, of course, it was a stupid dream.

It was possible — and she shuddered — that she carried a worthless girl-child. Yü could not believe that Princess of Streaked Clouds could be so cruelly unheeding. But if, indeed, the child in her belly was female, then she could not humiliate her Lord. The infant would be kept from his sight. Yü did not believe that her Lord would demand that the child be drowned in the Pei-ho. She had grown to understand him, and beneath his rough, blaspheming exterior there was softness. If the child was female, she would break its feet and bind them into tiny flowers, and her Lord would not be ashamed.

*

It had not been difficult to reach the *Simoom* in one of the dozens of sampans and lorchas that shuttled backwards and forwards with salt carcasses, crates of chickens, officers' wines from Dent's Canton warehouse, baggage and casks. A score of coolies swarmed the ship's deck, and nobody noticed Yü. It was dusk, and it was easy. She lowered herself among the nervous sheep, among the warm, greasy smell of them, clucking her tongue softly.

*

The troopship ploughed southward through a flat, brassy sea, pouring black coal-smoke into a clear sky. A blazing sun smote at the iron hull with the ferocity of a hammer, blistering the paintwork and caking salt along the waterline. Below decks the atmosphere was furnace-like, foul with the reek of sweating bodies, latrine buckets, and the fetid bilges. During the stifling dark hours the closely confined men lay sleepless and naked, cursing the burning rashes that flared at groin and armpits, the cockroaches, and the interminable salt rations that only added to a continuous, smouldering thirst. On deck, an awning had been spread aft for the officers, but elsewhere rails and bulkheads singed unwary flesh, the tar bubbled between the planks, and the boats were kept half filled with brine to prevent the seams from broaching.

When the *Simoom* dropped anchor in the harbour of Hong Kong, seven men were carried ashore, to die.

It was palpably clear that the ship, carrying a total of almost 1,300 persons, was overcrowded by even the callous standards of the Army. To proceed further, crossing the equator twice, under such conditions, could mean a death-toll of scores, and even the Army could not contemplate losing more men on a home-going voyage than in the campaign just fought. It was not that the Army was concerned overmuch with the comfort of the soldiers, but there could be critical editorials from the gutter-rakers of Fleet Street, and even questions in the House. The *Simoom* remained at anchor.

The brash new colony of Hong Kong, at the mouth of the Chukiang, the Pearl River, was a crowded anthill, the crossroads and clearing house of an Orient only now opening its reluctant doors to an avaricious, exploiting Europe. Wealthy ship-owners, merchants, bankers, agents and brokers rubbed shoulders with seamen from a dozen nations, rickshaw coolies, native fishermen, sweating redcoats and marines, roll-gaited Navy men, and a vast prostitute population — Chinese, English, French, Portuguese — and the wooden shanties of Happy Valley were surrendering place to brick-built bungalows, taverns, banking houses, whore-shops and warehouses. The first fine residences were appearing on the mist-shrouded Peak. From the mainland, beyond Kowloon, a continual, swelling stream of Chinese poured into the foreigners' territory, where laws were lenient, and there was money to be made. The vast harbour teemed with ships — tea clippers, opium steamers from India, frigates and shallow-draught gunboats, troopships, junks, floating brothels and fishing boats.

Anchored also off Victoria, loading tea, was the fast sailing ship *Flying Cloud*, anticipating a departure for England within the month. Sailing later than the *Simoom* intended to, and almost certainly with a less swift passage, the tea clipper's arrival might be five or six weeks after that of her coal-burning rival, but there was a percentage of the 60th Rifles whose rapid return home would be a matter of indifference to Whitehall. They were the time-expired men, the Indian 'yallers' whose service could be extended by two years if expiring on a foreign station. Four officers and 168 men were transferred to *Flying Cloud*.

Dando and Holloran stood in the waist of the anchored clipper, watching until the departing *Simoom* was a black smudge on the horizon southward. From the open holds behind them wafted a different aroma, of tea — Congou, Souchong, Orange Pekoe, Scented Caper, Young Hyson, Twankay, Imperial. It was an aroma they could tolerate.

Dando nodded at the empty China Sea. 'The bastard's gorn, Irish, an' I ain't bleedin' sorry. I ain't even sorry them 2nd Battalion griffins is goin' ter be swillin' quarts o' cold beer in Portsmouth a month before we are — them wot git ter Portsmouth.'

'Them thet *get* ter Portsmouth, bedad.' Holloran shrugged. 'Shure, they'll be naydin' ter take on extra bloddy coal et the Cape, fer weightin' orl the poor divils thet's buried et say.' He paused. 'Did I iver tell ye, me ol' Dando, ev the toim we orl went ter Jamie O'Connor's wake? There he wuz, bedad, as paceful as ye loik —'

17

In Latitude 18, two hundred miles eastward of the island of Hainan, the typhoon, the dreaded *tai-fung*, bore down upon the *Simoom* with the snarling ferocity of a tiger on a helpless roebuck. The glass had been falling for hours, followed by a ghastly flattening of the sea, a yellowing sky, and then the massive surge of the gale that heeled the vessel almost to her scuppers. On every deck, in every compartment, the holds, the bunkers, the cabins no larger than horse-boxes, men were flung, sprawling, among cascading baggage, arms and accoutrements, mess stores, and the deluging contents of hundreds of bags of coal stowed in every passageway and corner. Straining every rivet, the *Simoom* clawed herself, inch by inch, to an even keel. She had sprung in several places, the engine-room was awash with a foot of water, but her fires were still burning. Frantically her screws threshed — by God's grace powered by the oscillating geared engines of a frigate. She was built of iron; a wooden ship would have been torn to matchwood within minutes, but there was another, shuddering doubt. The *Simoom*, during her conversion from warship to troopship, had seen her vital thwart-ship bulkheads removed or pierced by doors, her backbone weakened. Had she the strength to sustain the crushing onslaught of a typhoon?

She had, only just. The dazed, sodden soldiers dragged themselves to the upper deck. Water swilled, shin-deep, everywhere, as the ship heeled again, sickeningly. The pens of sheep and goats, the crates of chickens and the bales of hay had disappeared over the side, while overhead the wind shrieked in the rigging. The sea, green and horrifying, thundered over the reeling deck, splintering into clouds of spume. The *Simoom* thrust her nose into the storm, seeming incapable of recovering, but she did, emerging again, slowly, slowly — her yards gone and broken cordage trailing and slashing. 'Remember the *Birkenhead*!' somebody shouted — and they remembered, uneasily — the *Birkenhead* that had foundered off Danger Point, with men of ten regiments standing in orderly ranks as the ship sank under them. It had been one of the proudest moments of the British Army — but who wanted to be reminded of the *Birkenhead*? Hadn't she broken in bleedin' 'arf, takin' 'undreds to their deaths?

To the north-east the sky was charcoal black, overhead the clouds low, heavy, and streaming with incredible speed before the gale. On the stern, seamen were fighting to lay out a storm anchor to help keep the vessel's bows to the sea, and amidships the bell was clanging like a child's toy. From the bridge the oilskinned captain roared orders through a voice trumpet, hugging a stanchion as the sea boiled over the side once again, the decks rearing and heeling crazily. The pumps clank-clanked, with sixty riflemen, struggling to maintain their footholds, pushing and tugging at the pump-bars. Another sixty hauled on wet, unfamiliar ropes to lift the boats free of their cradles, ready for out-hoisting.

*

The typhoon had passed on, south-westward, into the South China Sea, towards an unsuspecting Annamese coast. There was new warmth in the sun, and the *Simoom* wallowed gently, exhausted, in a long, easy swell.

Her upper deck was a shambles, still swilling with water in which floated sodden clothing, tangled ropes, the debris of deck cargo, and the pumps still clanked, as they had for hours. Men with reddened eyes, shivering, huddled in corners sheltered from the wind, fumbling for damp tobacco as the tired sergeants shouted their roll-calls. But the funnel was smoking bravely, and the cooks were coaxing life into the galley fires. There'd be an issue of rum, someone said, when they found some rum.

The First Lieutenant reported damage. The carpenter's party had plugged all leaks of consequence, and the pumps had won their battle. There was damage enough, but largely to the upperworks, and there would be no need to seek an unscheduled port for repairs. It was better than the captain had feared. 'And no lives, Number One?'

'It's scarcely credible, sir. The ship's company's all accounted for, and the Army say they've mustered every man. We've been damn' lucky. Apart from that' — he glanced at a crumpled paper — 'we've lost 23 sheep, 3 goats, 10 geese, 54 ducks and 132 fowls —'

The captain shrugged, turning back to the chart-table. 'We can re-stock at the Cape. In the meantime it'll have to be salt beef and preserves. Ye can call out the watch below to start clearing up that hog-sty of an upper deck —'

It was damn' odd, the First Lieutenant mused, as he made his way forward. It was bloody damn' odd. There wasn't a cussin' soul missing. But he'd *seen* a man go over the side — when that first green mountain of sea had torn the sheep pens and fowl crates from their lashings and hurled them, whirling, into the maelstrom beyond the lee gunwale. For a few fleeting seconds, through the stinging spume, he'd *seen* — and, dammit, the bo'sun had seen, too. They'd both shouted, helplessly —

He shook his head, confounded. Typhoons did bloody queer things to a man's faculties.

18

Across the harbour were the hazed hills of the mainland, the wide stretch of water scattered with lateen-sailed sampans, and lorchas — native hulls with European rigs — and trim naval cutters from the anchored warships, the frigates *Calcutta* and *Furious*, the gunboats *Coromandel*, *Beagle* and *Magicienne*. A tangled forest of masts fringed the wooden jetties, draped with drying nets stinking in the heat, swarming with flies, and piled with crates and casks, mounds of sacks and swollen baskets. The waterfront teemed with people — sweating, trotting coolies of both sexes, screeching urchins, seamen, sore-covered beggars, rickshaws, carts, occasional carriages.

In company with other clippers and steamships, *Flying Cloud* lay offshore, her holds battened, only hours from sailing, and stowing the last of her deck cargo before hoisting her Blue Peter. There had been rumours of cholera in the camp in Kowloon, and there was an anxiety to be gone from this fever-hole of Hong Kong, an anxiety for the clean, salt winds of the China Sea. Men knew how to fight hurricanes, and they'd take their chance with the blistering sun or numbing cold, with coastal pirates, fog, uncharted reefs, or vicious seas, but not cholera. Men couldn't fight cholera.

Queen's Road was a narrow, rutted thoroughfare, abandoned now by the better class Europeans and peopled mostly by Chinese, but also with a sprinkling of poor Whites, Eurasians, and outcast Portuguese from Macao. A few buildings showed evidence of thoughtful planning, but most were of ramshackle clap-board, sagging bamboo and rattan. There were *samshu* shops and gin shops, opium cellars, street kitchens, tattooists, gambling booths, and the inevitable, frequent brothels at which, at any hour of day or night, women of a dozen nationalities were readily available, jig-jig short time, jig-jig all night or, for that matter, all day, all week, for as long as the chink of silver continued.

Holloran eyed the anchorage uneasily. There were at least six junks lavishly painted with flowers and fishes, festooned with lanterns, swinging with the tide. 'Jasus —!'

Dando sniffed. 'It's 'undreds o' miles from the Pei-ho, ain't it? D'yer think them six wimmin are so 'ot wiv *impetuous*, they'd sail 'undreds o' miles, jes' fer a nibble wiv Patrick Holloran o' the 60th? If yer'd grown a beard, like I said, yer'd 'ave no bleedin' worry.' He sniffed again. 'Besides, we sail tomorrer — unless yer think they'll foller yer orl the soddin' way ter bleedin' Portsmouth?'

'Bedad, there's no knowin' wid bloddy wimmin,' Holloran spat. 'Wimmin is quare. Did I iver tell ye, me ol' jewel?' — he threw a glance over his shoulder at the crowded Queen's Road — 'Did I iver tell ye —?'

'Yer bleedin' goin' to, any minute,' Dando nodded. 'If it's pigs under the bed, or goats, or Molly Malone, or 'itting the goblin wi' the stew-pot, I've 'eard it before.'

The two men shared an inexplicable feeling of depression — inexplicable because in a few hours they would be at sea, bound for England and their discharge, an expectation that men clung to through years of detested service, praying that they would achieve it before being struck down by malaria, typhoid, or a Pathan bullet. Home-going drafts of time-expired men got themselves roaring drunk, and sang and blasphemed with joy, scoffed at the envious comrades they left behind, and boasted wildly improbable plans of civilian prosperity to come. It was a self-deception; the prospects of a discharged soldier were bleak. In the towns, even for skilled craftsmen, unemployment was widespread and work ill-paid, while rural labourers were impoverished and continually drifting into industrial areas to further swell the ranks of the employment seekers. A discharged soldier, with little to offer except ten or twenty years of military service, much of it overseas, would provoke scant interest. He might live by his wits, by crime, or he could sleep rough, and starve. Alternatively, when the winds of November plucked at his thin coat, and the rain soaked through his broken boots, he could seek a recruiting sergeant — of a different regiment because he feared the humiliation of returning to his first. He might even adopt a different name, and pretend to be a raw recruit — a stratagem that seldom deceived, but the sergeant would suck his teeth, say nothing, and give him the shilling.

'We cud hev a foight,' Holloran offered. 'Shure, we've not hed a good foight since Benares. Not a rale good bloddy foight.' But the suggestion lacked its usual enthusiasm.

'Or we could git bleedin' boozed,' Dando said, with equal indifference. 'We ain't goin' ter git boozed again fer four months, not on one tot o' rum that only sweetens yer spit.'

'Or wimmin?' Holloran added. The soldiers' repertoire was complete. Brawling, drinking, whoring. There was no further choice, unless they chose to sing hymns at a Mission meeting.

'Sod wimmin,' Dando pronounced. He had lost all desire for women. 'We'll git boozed, see? *Samshu.* It's cheaper'n beer, an' the gin's poison.' Sod wimmin. A man didn't need wimmin. Not reg'lar. A woman was a soddin' millstone. Never, he vowed, never take on a bleedin' woman —

'There'll be plenty o' tay,' Holloran mused. 'The shep's a bloddy floatin' tay-pot, so 'tis. Bedad, wid thet shep, ye cud bury the whole ev Donegal wid six fate ev tay, so ye cud.'

'Wot bleedin' for?' enquired Dando. Then he froze, and stood rigidly, staring.

A small Chinese woman, in nankeen smock and trousers, stood on tiny feet before them, her hands clasped. She bowed three times, her eyes lowered.

'My chin-chin you, one good flend. P'rhaps you come alonga me, look see, velly number one good ting?'

Dando choked. 'Christ! 'Ow the bleedin' 'ell —?'

She bowed again. 'You wanchee? You come, heya? Jig-jig short time, one dollar, plenty velly good.' She glanced at Holloran. 'Alla same one piecee flend, can do.'

From an open-fronted gin-booth, yards away, a party of tipsy sailors hooted. 'Ye'll need yer sea-boots, matey, an' a block an' tackle, if yer wants ter 'aul out alive. There's already two marines an' three stokers missin'. We only found their 'ats!'

'An' ef ut's throuble ye're after wantin' —!' Holloran roared, bouncing on his toes. 'Bedad, I'll give ye a bloddy mouthful ev knuckle! Did ye niver hear ev the Great Carnage ev Mag Muirthemme — ?'

The ragged rattan awning of the gin-booth heaved, and then collapsed, shredding underfoot. A flimsy wall shuddered and leaned crazily as the Chinese proprietor ran, shrieking at the sky, and an unfortunate rickshaw coolie, in mid-road, was flung sprawling with the splintered wreck of his vehicle. Dogs barked hysterically, bottles and glasses shattered, and blood-spattered men mauled and lashed, butted and hacked, fell to the ground and rose again, groggy but determined. Excited, nervous natives gathered at a safe distance, surging backwards and forwards as the battle moved from road to shop-front and from shop-front to road, wailing afresh as piled wares and cages of fowls tumbled and crashed under the lurching weight of the flailing fighters.

When the Buffs' provost patrol, summoned by the screeching of outraged Chinese, clattered into Queen's Road, they were met by a scene of utter ruin, of sagging awnings, splintered bamboo and smashed furnishings. The street was thickly scattered with fruit and vegetables from upturned baskets, tea bricks, rice and flour, slimed with broken eggs and spilt oil. Crazily fluttering fowls and ducks whirled a storm of feathers as a dozen small pigs ran, squealing, and a crowd of Chinese shopkeepers shouted abuse.

'Wid ye belayve ut!' Holloran spat disgustedly. He wiped blood from his face with a filthy hand. 'Kin a man niver hev a bloddy good foight widout the dooty picquet spoilin' everythin', bedad?' He turned to his panting opponent. 'Shure, an' ut's a foin fist ye hev, me bucko. Wid ye be givin' us the playsure ev ye' company in stretchin' these little red sodgers on their arrses —?'

But a provost patrol knew how to deal with drunks and brawlers — with rifle butts. Suitably battered, the two riflemen and four sailors were hauled to the jetty, where the seamen were surrendered into the unsympathetic hands of the *Calcutta*'s master-at-arms, who idly swung a knotted rope's end as he shouted for a Royal Marine escort. Fifteen minutes later, Dando and Holloran stood on the deck of the *Flying Cloud.*

'I might o' known it,' Sergeant Garvin nodded. 'I might o' known it. In ten soddin' years yer ain't been different. Drunk an' fightin'. The larst bleedin' day, an' yer *still* drunk an' fightin' —'

'Gawd strewth,' Dando snorted, 'we ain't 'ad a drop, Sar'nt — not a stinkin' drop! We was mindin' our own business, see —?'

'Shure, thet's roight, b'Jasus,' affirmed Holloran. 'We wuz moinding our own bus'ness, when harf the bloddy sailors ev the China Fleet comes changing down Quane's Road, drippin' wid rum an' roaring war an' dishtruction —'

The Sergeant nodded again. 'The Captain's given yer cells, as far as the Cape, on bread an' water. That's not less'n sixty days. As a special concession, yer kin 'ave a daily ration o' lime juice —'

*

'Bleedin' ecstatic, ain't it?' Dando decided. 'Sixty soddin' days on choke-dog an' water. Fer doin' nuthin'!'

'It wuz a bloddy good foight,' Holloran compensated. 'Es good es Benares.' He fingered his puffed and broken lips. 'Benares an' Hong Kong, bedad. Thim wuz the best foights we iver hed.'

They shared the small, iron-barred port-hole beyond which the distant wharves of Happy Valley were slowly receding as the *Flying Cloud*, under sail, turned her bows towards the open sea. It was November, 1861. They'd be in England in green April, and as they tramped through the streets of Gosport in their worn and faded regimentals, their faces lean and brown-burned, people would draw back from the kerb, and small boys would follow, hooting at them for Indians. When they had embarked from England, more than ten years earlier, London had been in the grip of the Great Exhibition fever. Since then much had happened. The Queen had borne her eighth and ninth offspring, Leopold and Beatrice, and the Navy had launched its last wooden ships, *Howe*, *Prince of Wales*, *Windsor Castle*, and *Victoria*, all of 6,930 tons, or twice the size of Nelson's *Victory*. France had been at war with Austria, Garibaldi had liberated Sicily and Naples, and Livingstone had discovered Lake Nyasa. Of greater consequence, the Civil War in America was already in its eighth month, and neither Dando nor Holloran, as the *Flying Cloud* took them from Hong Kong, could know that, at that moment, Britain was on the brink of war with the Federal Government of the United States, and British troops were already marching for embarkation to Canada. The Prince Consort would be dead before Christmas.

'It's bleedin' strange, ain't it,' Dando mused. 'We ain't fightin' nobody. No soddin' Russians or Chinamen, no Paythans. Not even any poor little bastard Kaffirs. If somethin' don't start agin nex' week, there'll be people writin' ter *The Times*, arskin' why there's so many idle, drunken gutter-scum o' soddin' redcoats, a constant drain on public bleedin' resources. Then they'll git the festerin' maps out, jes' ter see if there's any soddin' space that's not filled in yet, see? Burma, say, or Ashanti. Then orf we bleedin' go, wi' sixty rounds an' three days' soddin' 'ard tack, march ter the front an' don't lose yer dressin', aim fer the gut an' don't snatch, keep yer 'eads up, an' when they come at yer, give a rousin' cheer fer the bleedin' Queen.'

'Et's the truth, bedad,' Holloran agreed.

Bibliography

Bloodworth, D.: *Chinese Looking Glass*, Seeker & Warburg, 1967.

Bond, Brian: *Victorian Military Campaigns*, Hutchinson, 1967.

Butler, Lieut. Col. L.: *The Annals of the King's Royal Rifle Corps*, John Murray, 1926.

Carman, W. Y.: *British Military Uniforms*, Leonard Hill, 1957.

Edwards, Maj. T. D.: *Military Customs*, Gale & Polden, 1950.

Fortescue, J. W.: *A History of the British Army*, Macmillan, 1930.

Gardiner, L. P.: *English Historical Review*, Vol. XVI, Longmans, Green, 1901.

Hurd, Douglas: *The Arrow War*, Collins, 1967.

Latourette, K. S.: *The Chinese: Their History and Culture*, Macmillan, N.Y., 1964.

M'Ghee, R. J. L.: *How We Got to Pekin*, Richard Bentley, 1862.

Morse, H. B.: *International Relations of the Chinese Empire*, Longmans, Green, 1910.

Pemberton, W. B.: *Battles of the Crimean War*, B. T. Batsford, 1962.

Rennie, D. F. MD: *The British Arms in North China and Japan*, John Murray, 1864.

Rogers, Col. H. C. B.: *Troopships and their History*, Seeley Service, 1963.

Smyth, Sir John: *The Victoria Cross*, Frederick Muller, 1963.

Swinhoe, Robert: *Narrative of the North China Campaign of 1860*, Smith, 1861.

Williams, S. W.: *The Middle Kingdom*, Vol. II, Scribner, N.Y., 1899.

Wolseley, Lt. Col. G. J.: *Narrative of the War with China in 1860*, Longman, Green, Longman & Roberts, 1862.

Woodham-Smith, Cecil: *The Great Hunger*, Hamish Hamilton, 1962.

Printed in Great Britain
by Amazon